DREAMLAND

DREAMLAND

George V. Higgins

An Atlantic Monthly Press Book

Little, Brown and Company   Boston · Toronto

ATLANTIC-LITTLE, BROWN BOOKS
ARE PUBLISHED BY
LITTLE, BROWN AND COMPANY
IN ASSOCIATION WITH
THE ATLANTIC MONTHLY PRESS

LIBRARY OF CONGRESS CATALOGING IN PUBLICATION DATA

Higgins, George V 1939–
    Dreamland.

    "An Atlantic Monthly Press book."
    I. Title.
PZ4.H6365Dr   [PS3558.I356]   813'.5'4   77–4499
ISBN 0–316–88745–5

Published simultaneously in Canada
by Little, Brown & Company (Canada) Limited

PRINTED IN THE UNITED STATES OF AMERICA

Meet me in Dreamland,

Sweet dreamy Dreamland.

There let my dreams, come true.

DREAMLAND

I

IN THE late afternoon of the first Wednesday in September, two years ago, we were about three miles due east of Oak Bluffs, under power, heading home. The diesel hammered away below, creating noise and vibration just adequate to discourage conversation, and the boat wallowed along with the same sort of uncomfortable motion that an airplane makes when taxiing. The wind had been variable all day, around two or three knots, too light for us to use the sails, and we sat dispirited in the sunlight remaining of the summer.

Then as the sun descended, the wind picked up, first to a five-knot westerly, then to seven, finally settling from the southwest and holding the needle of the wind-speed indicator steady at twelve. Far enough from the immediate lee of the Vineyard to take some benefit from the breeze, Andrew headed her up into the wind. I went forward and set the mainsail, the great white triangle rising up the mast to flap in the wind, while Ellen on the port side of the cockpit urged the genoa furling line through the block as Deirdre brought the sheet through the starboard winch. Andrew swung the helm back and shut the engine down as the sails filled and we bore off on a long starboard tack against the ebb in Pollock Rip Channel. He took us to a heading of about ten degrees, and there was nothing to hear but the sound of the hull chafing through the water, the boat springing to balance on course for Nobska Point, surging forward on the wind and the current. I went aft to set the mizzen sail for stability, then paused for a moment, resting my hand on the mizzen boom, enjoying the light on the water, and the silence. When I returned to the cockpit, Andrew had begun, scratching around, almost idly, on the surface of assurances I had cherished all my life.

". . . with some suspicion," he said. "Now that by itself, of course, may not have meant as much to me as it should have, because I long ago became accustomed to Priddy's suspicion. The way people with piles get used to sitting funny — it's just this recurring kind of discomfort that comes along every so often, and there's nothing you can do about it, so you live with it. And you discount it, like a couple of rainy days in a two-week vacation.

"What I should have done," Andrew said, "was understand that when he came right out and said he was suspicious, he was downright unfriendly to the idea. And he was thinking as fast as he could — which, to be sure, isn't very fast, in objective terms, and accounts for my occasional success in outwitting him — to dream up some way to stop me from doing whatever it was that I'd mentioned to him."

During our first years in college, half a lifetime ago, I by chance encountered Andrew one night in the bar at Cronin's, off Harvard Square. I went there very seldom, but I had formed, in that first semester as a freshman, a friendship with John Thomas Laird, and tended for a while to follow his lead. Jack Laird came from the West Coast. He had spent several years as a pilot in the Navy, before resuming at Harvard the education he had interrupted after one year at the University of Southern California, and his comparative maturity and experience appealed to me at that stage in my life. The friendship did not last. Still when I learned, two or three years ago, that Jack Laird had been indicted in connection with the Sharpstown Bank manipulations, I was as saddened as I was grateful that my developing good judgment had caused me to drift away from him.

At any rate, I covered my surprise that night when we ran into Andrew, whom I would have expected to be hard at the books far away in Brunswick, Maine, and introduced him to Jack. Andrew, perfectly self-possessed, then introduced us to a gentleman whose name I have forgotten. He was about forty, I would say, a burly, quiet man, cursed with a very dark beard, transparent skin, and a large purple birthmark that began at the lobe of his left ear and extended over his cheek, around his eye, and up to his hairline. He wore a blue shirt, open at the neck, and a dark blue zipper jacket with a knitted collar. On the table in front of him was a large manila envelope, open, and next to it there was a stack of white cardboards with printing on them. He was extremely civil, but it was obvious that Jack and I had interrupted business, so after routine pleasantries, we adjourned.

When we were seated at our own table, I expressed my

perplexity that Andrew should be in Cambridge, and not at Bowdoin. "Very simple," Jack Laird said. "He's got the franchise there, obviously. He's picking up the cards for this week's games."

I never saw the man with the birthmark again. I never discussed the matter with Andrew. I did not, though it was with some concern, report the matter to my father, whose willingness to pay Andrew's tuition and living expenses might have been greatly affected had he known that Andrew was participating in a criminal gambling enterprise. But I remember that evening, and in later life I thought of it often as Andrew's ease in the midst of conflict impressed me again. "I can't stand quiet," he once said, reflectively. "When things get quiet, I get nervous. I think there must be something wrong. I'm not doing my job right. Something." My father, who learned in time of some of Andrew's other enterprises, once said that Andrew lived like a Bedouin.

"There was," Andrew said that September day on the boat, "some sentiment to the effect that Priddy was a perfect bastard to work for. When I first let it be known that I was going to the bureau, the guy I sat next to in New York looked at me and said: 'Gonna work for Michael Priddy, huh? I'd rather rub shit on my head.'

"My own opinion, after I got to know the guy," Andrew said, "was that Priddy wasn't bright enough to achieve perfection in anything. I had the poor judgment to express that position one day, while Priddy was prowling around outside his cage and passing the door to my cubicle. Which, as you might expect, made him even more suspicious of me than he'd been before. Distrustful, in fact. Hostile, even. If he could've canned me, he would've, and that night he would've gone home to kick the shit out of the cat in sheer joy, instead of, out of his usual filthy moodiness."

It had been hot that day, on the Sound, but in the wind and the declining sun, the temperature dropped. The perspiration, drying on our skin, made us chilly. Yet because Deirdre was there, I did not go below for sweaters, but resumed my seat in the cockpit, choosing the windward side because my sense of equilibrium is disturbed when I ride to leeward in a boat well heeled over in the water. Ellen, my wife, crossed her arms under her breasts, and hugged herself.

Ellen and I had known Deirdre only since the Fourth of July, when Andrew had brought her to Nantucket for her first visit. But that, and two more weekends, had been enough to instruct us that she was secure enough in the self-perception of her many excellences to indulge herself in several minor quirks sufficient to have prompted the rejection of a lesser mortal. She also knew of our fondness for Andrew (at the time, I thought she traded on it). She was capable of making acerbic remarks.

Accordingly, although I thought I had heard the story before — Andrew was in the process of educating her about people and events quite familiar to friends of twenty or thirty years, as though determined that she should know him as well as we did (a motive which I found as meritorious in concept as it was tiresome in pursuit) — I remained in the cockpit even though I was cold, and knew Ellen was, too. Deirdre, who seldom got cold, had established that she considered it a sign of weakness to admit to chilliness.

The wind continued steady from the southwest, and the seas, quartering, gradually increased to about two feet, so that we began to make some leeway, but Andrew, without mentioning it (perhaps without consciously adverting to what needed to be done), made the necessary correction of the helm. From where I sat, I could watch the boat swing until the lubber line of the compass in the chrome binnacle hung at two hundred and ninety degrees, and remained poised there. Andrew went on.

"In some ways, I suppose," he said, "Priddy probably had some reason for being the way he was. He had more prima donnas in that joint'n they ever saw at one time at La Scala. It was a very fast track he was in charge of running, and almost every one of us firmly believed what they said about us, when the roll was called up yonder on *Meet the Press,* or *Face the Nation,* or Martin Agronsky invited us in for a little light conversation. We knew we shouldn't believe it, of course, and each of us pretended that *he* was perfectly unaffected by it. Because, when you didn't, you got a whole ration of crap from the other guys. Who, naturally, believed it just as much as you did, but were better at concealing it, and making fun of it. Send in the clowns? Don't bother; they're here.

"It's a very competitive office," Andrew said. "It's got a tradition of being one. The night Priddy picked Coppersmith to do the sidebars on RFK's funeral, Martinelli almost had a fistfight with both of them. He thought he was the one that should've had it. When Martinelli went to China with Nixon, Coppersmith and Haley pouted for a week, and Norris was fairly sulky for three or four days. It's an addiction. It's also an economic fact of life: if you don't get a regular fix of the stuff that goes on the front page, you're not going to have anything to be insightful about on the Op Ed page, and ponderous about, for when you go down to the University of Duke, to talk to the journalism majors, twelve hundred bucks for gettin' hot licks, impressin' the girls."

I thought there was immediate regret for that remark, in the look that Andrew sneaked at Ellen. She was kind enough to keep her face open, though, with an expression of bright interest in his story. I still thought that I had heard it before, and I am sure that she thought she had, too. I therefore gave her full marks for being considerate, as I have had almost daily occasion to do, for close to seventeen years now. I have never been entirely convinced that she ever overcame her initial reaction to Andrew (or, for that matter, was sure that that reaction was inappropriate, and ought to be overcome), and I have always been convinced — indeed, it may have been my first glimmer of her steadfast intention never to provoke a dispute, or to permit one to continue, if someone somehow managed to begin one — that that reaction was unfavorable. No matter that she saw fit to deny it, and thereafter stuck to her denial.

"You like him very much," she said, the night that she first met him. It was another New England autumn evening, unusually warm, the darkness gathering earlier, reminding the heedful that the summer was over and the winter coming on, sixteen years ago, as I write this. Ellen and I had gone to the restaurant to celebrate the beginning of my second year in law school. My father, who had sponsored such observances, was unavoidably out of town, but had instructed the maitre d' to bill the charges to him. We were upstairs — the Men's Cafe, then, was still out-of-bounds to ladies except for the night of the Yale Game — and we encountered Andrew in the bar next to the Ober Room.

I envied him. He was lean and erect then, as he is now (I have kept myself in condition, I am glad to say, but I have, candidly, always envied him his height, and his sense of style in clothing), and he was justifiably full of his success; recalled from the London bureau of the Associated Press, he had been designated its principal correspondent for John F. Kennedy's campaign for the Presidency of the United States of America. He was twenty-two. His by-line ran on the front pages of newspapers around the world, and in the splendor of the dark wood paneling, the red and blue of the stained-glass windows, the white linens and the waiters in black tie serving Chambertin and filets of beef, he stood with one of the most beautiful women I have ever seen. Her name was Danielle. His eyes shone with satisfaction and the absolute confidence that there was more, much more, to come.

"I've known him for most of my life," I said to Ellen, when we had gotten home. "I don't know as I think much of her, though."

I am not an instinctual man. My father was not, and accounted it an advantage. He took the view that the Divinity had relented, in his case, from subjecting him to the distraction experienced by men of otherwise impeccable intelligence who suffer hunches, and sometimes act upon them. He was grateful for that favor.

I was never as confident of the rectitude of that view, but kept my own counsel until one night in April of 1972, when a coincidence of my business and Andrew's brought us to San Francisco at the same time, and we met for dinner at The Blue Fox. After more wine than was good for me, I found myself propounding Dad's position, to what premise I cannot possibly imagine.

Andrew has blue eyes, and they are deeply set. He has a mannerism in which he employs them, and I should imagine it to be of considerable usefulness to a man in his line of work: seemingly intent upon something else (that night, a breast of duck, Montmorency), he feigns — I am sure he feigns — startled interruption of an unrelated train of thought. As though struck by a flash of insight which you gave him, probably did not mean to give him, and will certainly live to regret giving to him, he snaps his head up and bores into your eyes with his.

It is disconcerting, as is any trick perfected by long practice. I seem to recall him manifesting that trait as a child, in games

on the sloping lawn of the house in Duxbury, a discombobu-
lating trick, the more effective because no matter how many
times it has been played upon you, nor however you have
remarked it, and prepared yourself for its eventual re-perfor-
mance, it always rattles you again.

"Yeah," he said, that night in San Francisco, "hunches. You
know what he told me? 'Never draw to an inside straight.' I
was about nine years old then. Didn't know what in the name
of the bloody blue Jesus he meant by it."

Andrew then resumed his operations on the duck, chewing
like a ruminant, looking off into the middle distance, finishing
the trick more ostentatiously than necessary, affording his victim time to recover from the tactic; it tempts one to conclude
that its performance was an accident, that nothing is wrong,
and so to set the stage for the next refinement.

"By the time I was old enough to know what it meant," he
said, in the ivory and blue of the mirrored restaurant, "I had
forgotten that he said it. By the time I remembered that he'd
said it, I'd been doing the opposite for a number of years, and
I'd grabbed a considerable number of pots from people who
assumed I'd improved two pair to a full boat, when all I really
had was a busted straight."

He looked down at the plate and speared another piece of
duck, coated with the black cherry sauce. He put it into his
mouth, regarded me and chewed, swallowed, taking calm sur-
vey to be sure that he'd unbalanced me.

"By then it was too late to quit." He drank some wine. "Ever
get reckless enough to try it, Dan?"

That is the finish of the trick: the question fired while you
are still off-balance, the one intended to obtain what he pretended to have secured from the chance remark that he employed as his cue. I venture to say that there are probably
several men of prominence who grieve to this day the extra

few milliseconds they spent in the erroneous notion that they had already given something away, and might as well do the best they could to recover from having done it, only to give away precisely, by that effort, what Andrew Collier had been seeking in the first place.

I do not gamble, and he knows it. I need exercise no great effort of will to abstain from it. As I have said, I share my father's advantage or deficiency, whichever it may be. And I always have, which may perhaps explain why he perceived no obligation to afford me any instruction whatsoever in what Andrew calls the holy game of poker. Dad sensed my reservations about the advantageousness of mutations of the instincts, and knew that I would probably never play the game. Andrew knew, or at least suspected, that I never had. As I recall, I did not answer Andrew that night in San Francisco. I did not have an answer that I cared to give.

It is because, in fact, that I am not an instinctual man, that Ellen is so valuable to me. That night in Locke's in 1960, when I said I had some reservations about Danielle, Ellen tried to draw me out, a process which I must confess that I resisted. She asked me why I was put off by Danielle, and I said I did not know. I groped for reasons, shying away from expression of what was certainly the main one:

Danielle was stunningly, breathtakingly, beautiful. She had large gray eyes. She had ash-blonde hair. She was of medium height, and had a very attractive figure. She wore a black dress with ruffles at the neckline, and while it was not extreme in *décolletage*, it did not need to be. Her jewelry was scant, impeccable and expensive. Her voice was cultivated; she was clearly well-educated.

Such women, then, had always intimidated me. I resented them because I wanted them, and I was afraid to seek them because I knew they would reject me. I thought they would reject me. This is painful for me; suffice it to say that I did not approach them.

"I don't know," I said to Ellen. "I just think there's something wrong there."

"You," Ellen said. "I think she's first-rate. She's desperately in love with him, and perfect for him, too. I only hope he doesn't think it's just because he deserves her."

I pressed Ellen, then, about her reaction to Andrew, and found her at least as evasive as I had been about my reaction to Danielle. We went to bed that night in mingled amusement and frustration. "Counsellor," she said, smiling, "your claim for immediate relief is granted."

She conferred upon Andrew that day in September, fifteen years later, the same sort of consideration. In the years that came between the night at Locke's, when Kennedy was facilely promising to get the country moving again, and the shag end of 1971, she became and remained fast friends, though at considerable distances, with Danielle Harkness Collier. When Andrew and Danielle were divorced, in May of 1972, Ellen said only that she intended to remain friendly with Danielle, a resolution as firm in its making as mild in its statement.

Andrew did not then demur, quite certainly because he knew he did not have to, nor did he care to, if he had been so obliged. But Andrew is crafty. He knew it was a resolution, one of very, very few, that he could greatly complicate in Ellen's efforts to carry it out. And he did so.

Nantucket is a small island. Ellen considered that ordinary delicacy forbade simultaneous association with Andrew and Danielle (I am not by any means certain that she was correct in that judgment, but I deferred to it). Since Andrew's visits, always in the company of other women, were, while brief, fairly frequent, and always unpredictable, it was hard for Ellen to arrange for summer visits with Danielle. At least that was the explanation which she gave, with a sadness so evident that I marveled at her generosity in tolerating spending so much of our time with Andrew, and the women who serially replaced Danielle.

Once he was divorced — perhaps, for all I know, before — Andrew demonstrated an avidity for women which startled his recent friends. It wasn't new, but its open ferocity was. Ellen called it "the heartbreak of satyriasis," laughed at him and pitied him. But there was hurt reserved beneath that forgiving exterior, and with it, too, a disapproval which though she forebore to express it, burdened her more than Andrew, even, could ignore. And that was why he sneaked that look at her, after mentioning impressing the girls.

"It must be tiresome," she said, sympathetically.

The Vineyard, by then, was low and greenish-gray in the residual sunlight, which dazzled our eyes when we looked to the west. But the light at Nobska Point stood white and clear. We were on Andrew's course.

"Ma'am," Andrew said, in an exaggerated imitation of a Louisiana drawl (another of his irritating affectations; he told me once that he acquired it while in the main office of the newspaper — because so many of its executives were Southerners, they could be baited quickly and successfully by mocking their inflections), "it's a perfect *bitch*, but it sho' do pay lahk de dickens.

"Well," he said, "in my catlike way, I of course seen at once that Brother Priddy had a gigantic hair across his ass about the ideah I'd done proposed to him." He chewed on an imaginary straw. My skin began to tighten as the sun- and windburns took effect, and I was cold. Ellen remained attentive. Deirdre showed telltale signs of wanting a nap. Andrew, at six-one, one-sixty, fought the wheel successfully, his knuckles reddening and then whitening only when he relaxed for a moment against the force of the leeway, then gripped the wheel to bring the boat back. His wrists were thin. He did the job with leverage, not force.

Deirdre got up. At twenty-eight, she looked perhaps six years younger. She had long black hair. "Down to her ass," Andrew had said, when he introduced her. "This is Deirdre. You will notice that she's got hair down to her ass." And she had smiled and said: "Andrew's so coarse. It's only long enough to cover my boobs."

I was somewhat surprised that she stood up. From the corner of my eye, I could see that Ellen was similarly puzzled. Deirdre was always almost embarrassingly attentive to Andrew's stories; if one person, in a group of several, could unilaterally create a hush when another spoke, then that is what Deirdre did when Andrew talked.

"Y'all goan take a *leak*, honey?" Andrew said.

"Nope," she said, stretching in the cocoa-brown bikini, to considerable erotic effect, "I'se jes' gwine below, fo' few minutes." Another of Andrew's irritating affectations: he always trained his ladies in them too, so that they seemed, interchangeably, to be part of a cheap vaudeville act. "Y'all jes' tote de barge. I'll lift de bale."

She went below. Andrew, smiling at her back vanishing down the companionway, said: "I'd jes' soon try out a little Jim Beam on this thang, long's you're up, honey."

I was about to ask for a beer, and I believed that Ellen would have welcomed one also. But as I opened my mouth to say so, Deirdre turned on the companionway stairs, looked over her shoulder, and said: "*In* the Hole. *After* the bridge. *When* we're in the Eel Pond. *Then* you can have one." She shifted her gaze, first to Ellen, then to me. "You guys want a beer?"

"Yup," Ellen said.

"Me too," Deirdre said. When she emerged from the companionway, she carried three cans of Carling's in her hands, and two windbreakers, for Ellen and me. I studied her face for malice, and I found none.

II

THEN I LOOKED at Andrew. Not immediately, of course. It would have been far too obvious that I expected him to react angrily to Deirdre's insubordination, and Andrew has a practice of gratifying people's expectations in such matters. Sometimes he distorts what they anticipated, in order to add an extra measure of unpleasantness. Andrew, I learned early, has a volcanic kind of anger.

On his eighth birthday, several years before he managed to develop any temperance at all in the governance of his disposition, he exploded in a rage which I can still remember, vividly.

Because his birthday is June fifteenth (1938; mine is August fourth, 1938), we always celebrated it at Duxbury, with a party on the lawn when the weather was nice. I would have preferred to have been born in the winter, because that would have enabled me to celebrate in Milton, and my chums from school would have been available. But in summer, of course, all were scattered to the winds. Greeley and Favor went to Bar Harbor, Bryce to Boothbay, Connors and Fish to Chatham and Nantucket, respectively. So our birthdays were family parties, with tables set up under the tall maples where the lawn fell away toward the harbor and the statue of Myles Standish, across the water in Plymouth, stood in the clear air.

For all his kindness, my father was an austere man, a very austere man. And a physically imposing one, too, which made him seem to me, at least as a boy, somewhat forbidding. He kept himself in trim, at the same weight — one-seventy-two — that he had reached when he was boxing at the college (he graduated in '19).

He did not marry until he had attained the age of thirty-five; by then, in the course of establishing his fitness to succeed to my grandfather's place in community, state and national affairs, he had altogether pretty much completed the formation of his character.

He had a gravity of manner, and a reticence in the expression of any strong emotions which he may have felt, which made him the more severe in aspect. Hard work, too, had left its traces on his features.

All of the males in our line have lost their hair, except for a few sparse strands, by the time that they were thirty years old; my father was long since past possible mistake as a contemporary, or playmate, when I was born. My grandfather, Daniel Carson Wills, '81, having followed the same course to which he had persuaded my father, was in demonstration of emotion all but indistinguishable from Dad. I believe that Dad, before I was born, neither extended to, nor received from, his father, the sort of fond affection which Ellen rightly believes to have been so constructive in the upbringing of our boys. But it was very difficult for me, even being much younger when my children were born, than they were when theirs were brought into the world, to master the practice of showing love and esteem to children by embracing them and kissing them.

My father, I believe, was conscious of his deficiency. I think he also knew that his bearing and manner were somewhat more than necessarily confirmatory of his preference for courtesy and good behavior. I think he tried, as best he could, to mitigate the effects. He was energetic and elaborate in his arrangements for the observation of holidays and other happy occasions in the family.

At Christmas, the public rooms in the house at Milton were festooned with laurel, holly, evergreen and mistletoe, and there were great wreaths, with ribbons of red and green tied into lavish bows. There were candles and puddings and large silver bowls of eggnog, and punch. We observed Christmas in what I now perceive to have been a mingling of traditions from New England and from London, my father recalling his years abroad, and taking from them what he had seen and heard and tasted, in London, before the war. The best of their traditions, to blend with our own.

There were, for example, coins in the heavy puddings, prepared by Cook in August, while we were still ensconced at Duxbury. Great elation was expected of the lucky diner who received a slice that contained one, steeped in brandy for more than four months, topped off with a wonderful hard sauce — he would enjoy good luck for the coming year. Somehow, both Andrew and I always received a slice with a coin, and never thought it strange that my father's disappointment at not receiving one, was so plainly put on.

At the same time of the year, there were rides in the sleigh behind Hester, through the silence of the Blue Hills, broken only by the crunch of the runners on the frozen surface of the snow, and the light, happy sound of the bells on Hester's harness. Mrs. Collier (Betsey, Andrew's mother) saw to it that we were all bundled up when we set forth to see the spruces clothed in snow and icicles, and the small tracks of animals around the smaller bushes, first the sunset, then the early moonlight filtering through the branches of the pines and evergreens. When we got home, there were steaming refreshments to warm us, and a twelve-foot hemlock stood in the foyer, decorated with cranberries and popcorn and ribbon garlands, the gifts piled high beneath.

We were such a happy tribe in those days, and now it seems so long ago. True, our life's more streamlined; as though in obedience to vast improvements in our transportation, we had decided also to make better speed in the rest of our lives, and thus to do more. But I wonder if we have not lost more than we bargained for, abandoning so many of our traditions.

Now, when Memorial Day arrives to herald the summer, Ellen and the boys and I attend the parade in Lexington. Then we return to Lincoln for a leisurely brunch with the Fields. That is the whole of it.

When I was a boy, there was a tingling of anticipation on that day. It was the last big day (full of excitement, of course, since the war was so recently over) at home. Mother would soon direct that the white cotton covers be brought down from the attic, and call for the men to come for the rugs to be cleaned and then stored, for the summer we would shortly commence in Duxbury. There has been a loss of meaning, a diminution of occasions in which sentiment was expected, and a reduction of excitement, brought about by the very multiplication of devices and diversions frantically concocted to create new forms of it.

Andrew does not share that view. I have never asked him, and I do not need to do so. The real wax candles burning in the evening; the slow and somehow-gratifying growing of awareness that my normally reserved father had permitted himself several whiskies, and was actually becoming somewhat jovial; the joyfulness in the way that my mother bustled about the house, and laughed when he captured her under the mistletoe; Andrew's mother's sadness when it was time to remember the Fallen, with Taps after three volleys on the Green (I always sneaked a look at Betsey in the sunlight, then, and, when she bowed her head, I was sure that she was saddened and embittered by the awful loss that she had suffered at El Alamein, where, Dad told me, Andrew's father had been killed): none of these things ever seemed noticeably to impress Andrew, and if today he were accused of not regretting them, I am sure that he would cheerfully concur. He prides himself, I think, on lack of feeling.

Reflecting on it now, in fact, it comes strongly to me that I have always known that Andrew never really joined in, never really took part in the happy events that included him, or at least were carefully arranged so that he might be included. He did not by any means spoil all of them, or even very many of them, by displays of anger. But he was ferret-eyed in his watchfulness at Christmas, and on my birthdays and his own, examining the presents that each of us received, and making mental inventories to determine whether he should feel that he'd been fairly treated by comparison. He always had been, of course; my father saw to that, tirelessly and futilely attacking a resentment that remained impervious to anything that he could do.

I can only speculate, of course, on the origins of Andrew's attitude. But I remember vividly the first occasion when his unreasoning emotion broke the surface. It was June fifteenth, 1946, and I was permanently appalled by the violence of Andrew's anger. *Temper* is a word most commonly misused; Andrew, then, did not have a wicked temper — he had no temper at all, and what little he has now he obtained only after many devastating, self-induced calamities at last brought him to the realization that he was ruining his life, and doing it himself.

I had gone into the house that sunny afternoon, so that I missed the beginning of his tantrum. While I am sure that Mother, or someone, later satisfied my curiosity about what had upset him, it must have been when I was sleepy. Or else the explanation is simply that it was so long ago; I have never retained things I have heard as well as I remember things that I have seen.

I was emerging from the white door of the cedar-shaked cottage (I can remember that house still, as it was, the bay window in the library, blue pillows on the buff cushions against the dark brown wood of the settee, the chess table with the sterling silver pieces left in position for the instant in the evening when I'd resume my game with Dad, thirty minutes before bedtime; he always beat me, until I was about ten, explaining carefully that he played as well as he could so that I would learn to play as well as I could, and thus, some day, play better than he) when I heard the commotion. I was eight then, I insisted, although in fact I would not be, for another two months, and I was wearing white flannel shorts and a blue blazer. On the lawn by the table where the adults sat with their refreshments, Betsey was crouching in front of Andrew. He was rubbing his eyes; my mother and father, deliberately disregarding Andrew and Betsey, were chatting in the shade. My father wore a blazer like mine, and white flannel trousers. He was drinking lemonade, and a cicada sang in the early summer heat. Off to the left, in a place where the lawn was level, the older children played croquet, avoiding the rhododendron bushes where the honey bees congregated. Two of

Andrew's special friends from town stood awkwardly nearby, with their hands in their pockets, distressed and uncertain about what to do.

I saw that he was upset, and I was concerned. I ran down the lawn toward him and his mother. He was berating her. "No, you *don't*," Andrew said.

"I do, Andrew," she said. I loved Betsey then, and I was grieved when she succumbed to illness back in 1967. I was also angry at Andrew, although I never mentioned it to him: she had moved back to Cambridge, England, four years before, and I did not hear of her passing, or even of her disability, until long after she was dead, because Andrew did not see fit to tell me. "She was sick and she was old, and all her friends were dead," he said, when I called to express my sympathy. "I saw her last summer and she was failing. I made her go to the doctor, and I went with her, myself. He told her what she had to do to get the blood pressure down, and he gave her anti-coagulants, and she told him, with me sitting right there, that he could prescribe anything he wanted, but she wasn't going to take it."

I was shocked. Betsey was only about fifty years old when she died.

"She thought she was old," Andrew said. "She had a hard life for a woman. Hell, a hard life for anybody. Her father got killed in the First World War. She never had a dime to her name. Somebody or other got killed in the Second World War, which left her alone with me, still without a dime. You can call it what you want, Dan, but she didn't bring me to Milton because she thought the streets of America were paved with gold — she emigrated because she couldn't do anything but take charity, and what Cable offered was the best charity she could get. But if you think she liked taking handouts, when she should've had better things by right, you're mistaken. Sadly mistaken. She was proud, and it didn't do her one damned bit of good. Hurt her, in fact, taking slops and leftovers in a foreign country. When she went home, she was just admitting it, finally. That she was defeated."

I remember the night that Betsey went home. We had a party for her at the house in Milton. My father, Ellen and I were crushed by her decision, and so in fact was she. We wept, for we loved each other. My father gave her her tickets, a check for five thousand dollars, and assured her that his accountants would remit to her each month, for as long as he lived, half of the salary he had paid her. She was very appreciative. She said that she was going home because she had finished her work with us, and wanted to do something else. There was not the slightest suggestion of bitterness, and we sat by the fire in the library and drank her health in champagne.

I did not argue with Andrew. Betsey did it, that day of his eighth birthday party. "I do love you, Andrew," she said to the little boy. "We all do. This party is for you."

"I didn't get anything I wanted," he said, still crying as I approached. "You didn't get me anything I wanted." He was small for his age — I was rather stocky, I must admit — but he was troublesome despite that, and I saw that she was holding each of his wrists. She was a woman of average height and weight (she was pretty, too), but she had difficulty preventing him from lashing out with his little fists. He was very strong for such a small boy. "You hate me," he said, and tried to get free.

"*Andrew!*" she said, and in her dismay released her grip on his left wrist just enough for him to jerk it free. He formed a fist and hit her, squarely on the nose, and while the force of the blow was not enough to cause her to lose balance as she crouched, the shock of receiving it from her little son evidently was. She toppled off, silently for a moment, toward her left, away from me, and I saw, as I came close to Andrew, my father rising slowly, in disbelief, from his lawn chair.

I have always thought that I could help. I thought so as a child, and there are times, even now, when I catch myself in that frame of mind and must sternly admonish myself that what happened then, and many things that have happened since, plainly demonstrate that it is not always so, and should have cured me of that notion.

"Andrew," I said, rushing up to him.

He turned on me. His face was distorted, red from crying, and from rage. "You did it!" he screamed. "You did it. You made her hate me." Then he rushed at me, fists clenched.

I really had no trouble fending him off. I was doing so quite nicely, saying: "Andrew, Andrew, I don't want to hurt you." But my father, by then, was behind him. Dad stooped, picked him up under the arms, and started carrying him off to the house, while Andrew screamed how much he hated Dad, too. At the steps, with the noisy child held well away from him in order to avoid the kicks that Andrew aimed at his privates, Dad said: "Francis and Tommy" — they were Andrew's friends — "Andrew's party is over. He is going to bed. You can see him next Friday."

With their heads down, they shuffled off down the drive, and I stored away the fact that while Andrew might be free of house arrest in six days, he would probably retain his capacity for ventilating his rage upon whomever was handy when he went into it. I have never forgotten it. I had never seen such behavior before. I played croquet solemnly with the other younger guests, and engraved what I had seen upon my brain.

In the boat that day, two years ago, with the evening coming on and the summer almost gone away, the sky becoming deeper, deeper blue and the wind thrumming in the leeside rigging, I looked at him with what I hoped was an expression of innocence. It might be that he was disinclined to become angry at Deirdre, but would, if exasperated, transfer his fury to Ellen or to me, and I therefore sought not to provoke him.

He was smiling. He was full of ease. "Y'all know, honeychile, you're prolly raht." I never did know what to expect of Andrew.

III

HE RESUMED, as we left Oak Bluffs off the port stern in the dying light, Ellen and I in our windbreakers, Deirdre apparently comfortable in her skimpy bathing suit, Andrew himself at the sort of peace with the world available only to a raconteur with a captive and attentive audience. The wake was straight and true, the landmarks at Falmouth precisely where he wanted them to be, and while the seas were regular, we did not pound or porpoise. I reached for a throwable life preserver cushion, and offered it to Ellen. She leaned forward on the port side of the cockpit, and I placed it behind her. She leaned back again, and thanked me with a smile. She had always loved sailing, and always loved me, even when those things have obliged her to put up with Andrew, his coarseness and his moods.

"Being an extremely unimaginative sort," Andrew said, "Priddy's first reaction to any proposal that I make is to say it's gonna be too expensive." He, too, leaned back, threw his head back, laughed, and straightened up again. "Now generally, Priddy's dead right, when he says that. There ain't no question about it: Mike Priddy is dead right many more oftens'n he's dead wrong about what it's gonna cost for me to do something for the World's Greatest Newspaper. Which is *not*, honey," he said, addressing Deirdre, "the gawdamned *Chicago* fuckin' *Tribune*, lahk yo' old daddy done brung you up to believe." Deirdre smiled.

Deirdre, as we knew by then, was born and raised in Chicago, in an outrageously expensive apartment on the Loop. The youngest of three daughters, she had been indulged furiously by her father, who had obtained a divorce, and custody of the children, from her mother when Deirdre was six. We had commiserated with her.

"He was right," she said. "And not just because he said he was right, either. I've seen her a few times, since I was old enough to go and see her on my own — she seldom bothered to come around and see me — and she's a goddamned tramp. That's all. Not a whore, not a hooker, not a call-girl, not even a cocktail waitress. Just a goddamned tramp. She turned into one. She's been married and divorced three times since my father threw her out in disgust, and the last time I saw her — she's about fifty-one, to be exact — she'd gotten married again.

"This is a woman," Deirdre had said, "who refuses to learn from experience. She got married to my father, and she ran around on him, and I guess she did the same thing, more or less, to every other fellow that she married. All I know is that she was living apart from her fifth husband, broke as usual, begging me for dough — which I used to give her, never stopping to think it was my father's money she was scrounging off me — going to beauty parlors and running up bills, chasing another man.

"The only man she wants," Deirdre said, "is the man she hasn't got. No, that's wrong. The only man she *doesn't* want is the man she's got. Far as I know, the only one she ever got a penny from was my father, and you know what that soft-hearted son of a bitch is *still* doing, twenty years later, and four husbands? He's paying for it. If I hadn't taken advantage of him so many times myself, I'd tell him how she's taking advantage of him."

I told her, that day in July, that her father seemed like a very nice man.

"I'll tell you what my father is," she said, "I can tell you right off. He's harder on himself'n he is on anybody else, and it's not because he's nice, or even generous; it's because he's got nothing but contempt for people like her. He thinks she's hopeless, and he knows he's not. So, when it got to the point where he knew it'd be better for all of us if he just threw her out, hired a housekeeper, and cut his losses, he threw her out, got a housekeeper, and did the best he could. And it was pretty good. At least I think it was, and you know how I've repaid him?" We did not, of course. "Well," she said, "let me put it this way: I'd kill for him."

She had graduated from a private school near Chicago. Neither Ellen nor I had ever heard of it. She had graduated from the University of Wisconsin, worked briefly for Batten, Barton, Durstine & Osborn in their Manhattan office — training, I gather, for work in television accounts — and became impatient. Through a college friend, she then found a job with the Institute for Policy Studies, in Washington.

"I didn't like that, either," she said. "I was bored speechless by those people. I guess they knew what they were doing, but it didn't interest me at all. For lack of anything better to do, I got married to the guy I was living with. Which will not be included in the list of the twenty best decisions I have ever made. When I left the job, I had to leave him, too."

I am reciting this because she said it, and a good deal more, too. Neither Ellen nor I solicited the confidences which we received from Deirdre Tinker. But we heard about her love affairs, the problems she had in securing her divorce, and how she felt when her father was indicted for falsifying loan applications in his capacity as an executive vice president of Midlands Fidelity Trust. All Ellen did was ask her, casually, where she had met Andrew, and she answered: "He picked me up at the Café Royal, in London," and went on from there.

After her divorce — Deirdre had rejected alimony, she said, which made me wonder if she might be, perhaps, more like her mother than she thought — she had lived for a while on savings, and the income from a small trust. Then, while considering application for unemployment compensation, she landed a job with the Foreign Service, which she retained. She was vague about her duties. She was on extended leave. "I was tired," she said. "I'd piled up all this leave, and it was time to come home." I was sure that she had not given the real reason.

We decided on the running lights as the Elizabeth Islands loomed dark off the port, and we ran for the Hole. I inquired whether Andrew wanted me to relieve him. "I thought you might be getting tired."

"Nope," Andrew said, at the helm. "When I find myself in times of trouble, Mother Mary calls to me, speaking words of comfort, let it be, let it be."

He thought, I am sure, that I did not know what the words meant, which demonstrated his assurance of a sole acquaintance with a broad spectrum of experience. I have sons in their early adolescence, and long ago determined to remain conversant with varieties of cipher. It did not surprise me, to be by implication patronized for ignorance, or, in the alternative, simultaneously derided for lacking it, but disapproving of the practice which I knew about. But the surest consequence of rising to bait put out by Andrew, is to be baited, again and again and again. I said nothing.

I think — I hope — he was disappointed. Collecting himself, he went on. " 'Mister Priddy,' I said, 'it's gonna cost like the bloody devil, and there's not a *thang* in the world that I can do about it. If you think it's worthwhile, talking to the man, you gotta send me where the man is, that's willing to talk.'

" 'You're forgetting, I think,' Priddy said, 'that I can also send somebody else.' "

I was not alert. I had heard, before, Andrew's stories about his continuing conflict with Michael Priddy, whom I had never met, but rooted for, silently, each time I heard one. Priddy was always the villain, and the buffoon to boot. Andrew was always the victor. Some day, just once, I hoped to hear a story in which Priddy deservedly won, and Andrew, having made a fool of himself, lost. I did not really expect to hear such a story from Andrew, if, indeed, such an exchange had ever occurred (if even a tenth of Andrew's stories about Priddy were true, then Priddy was the fool that Andrew claimed he was, venturing into combat, time and time again, with a subordinate, only to lose as many times as he had, and if that was so, then there was no Priddy-as-victor story); I just hoped for it.

The fact of the matter was that Andrew was extremely proficient at his job. That did not make it easier for me to endure the retelling of his coup of interviewing Francis Gary Powers before anyone else managed it, on the strength of his friendship with James Donovan, the lawyer who arranged the swap for Rudolph Abel in Berlin. Andrew located Che Guevara, and interviewed him high in the Bolivian mountains, or in Chile, or in some such place. Andrew glimpsed and recognized Carl Furillo of the Brooklyn Dodgers, on a construction job within blocks of Andrew's office, and obtained one of the most poignant interviews that I haver ever read. The finish to that story was: "Priddy, it cost you subway fare. Right in your league. Plus, of course, my exorbitant salary." Andrew convinced Priddy that he should be sent to the South Pacific, when he needed a vacation, to look for a crank who claimed to know the location of Amelia Earhart's plane. Andrew found the man, and he did not know. "Just another old bum of the islands," Andrew said, "who happened to have been a navy ace four times over, a Rhodes Scholar, and the best human interest story I think I ever did."

I am a practicing attorney. I have great faith in precedent.

"No," Andrew said, "I told him: 'No, you can't send somebody else. You can wish that you could send somebody else, but you can't do it.' " The twilight accumulated, the sea working against the hull, the hull against the sea and the force of the wind. " 'I'm the only guy in the world that he'll see.' "

It was too dim, by then, for Ellen to catch any of the private Oh-my-God signals that we've developed, over the years, to alleviate shared boredom by acknowledging, to each other, that we shared it. Had there been light enough, as we went into the Hole, I probably would not have risked one.

"Oh, my God," Deirdre said, getting up.

"What?" Andrew said, sounding a little offended.

"Not you," she said. "I'm finally cold." And she started below.

"A jacket for me, sweetie?" Andrew said.

She paused on the stairs again, and turned around. In the twilight we could see her smiling.

"I thought it was 'sweetheart,' " she said.

"Nope," he said, "that's when I want Rewrite."

She said: "Oh," and vanished into the gloom. I saw the flashlight come on — we saved the batteries underway, when the engine was off — and the beam of it precede her into the forward cabin.

"Well," Andrew said, "he didn't believe me."

I cautioned him. "Wait a minute," I said. "Deirdre won't know what the hell you're talking about."

"She's already heard it," Andrew said. "Only happened last week." He made a conciliatory gesture toward me with his right hand, extending his arm, the hand palm upward, to show he held no weapon. "Gimme a chance, willya?"

"Sorry," I said.

"It was true, for once, what I said to Priddy," Andrew said. "It was absolutely true. The others, they would've talked to somebody else with my credentials, *and* the World's Greatest Newspaper, if they had gotten there first. I just got there first. But this one actually got in touch with me, and demanded me, personally, and wouldn't talk to anybody else, and said so."

"Who the hell was it?" I said.

"Remember the lame man?" Andrew said.

I did not.

"General Gammage," Andrew said.

I still did not.

"At your father's funeral," Andrew said. And then, after considerable difficulty, I started to remember.

$$\boxed{\text{IV}}$$

TECHNICALLY, Andrew was wrong, and probably deliberately so. Wills men do not have funerals.

For my father, Daniel Cable Wills, we obeyed his wishes, and the traditions established at the death of my great-grandfather, Daniel Millis Wills. They were followed also for my grandfather, Daniel Carson Wills.

Perhaps I should explain, at this point, another of our family traditions. For five generations, the firstborn male offspring of a Wills male has been given the first name *Daniel*. His middle name is his mother's maiden name. Those conversant with our family distinguish between father and son by addressing us by our middle names. To them I am known as "Compton," or "Compton Wills," because my mother was Carolyn Anne Compton, of the Ipswich Comptons. My elder son is called "Hadley." His younger brother, David, is referred to by the diminutive of the same middle name: "Lee."

Nominally, I suppose, the Wills males have been Episcopalians. We annually attend Easter and Christmas services at Trinity Church and as a matter of course contribute each year the sum of one thousand dollars to the pastoral fund. But the place to which we return, on all occasions of happiness or sadness, is the chapel at the College.

"We do not bring our dead there," my father instructed me, when I was about fifteen and he judged me mature enough to undergo preparation for my probable duties at the time of his decease. While the women in the Wills line have retained their affiliations with the churches in which they were raised, and have ordinarily chosen interment with their families, Wills men direct their sons to arrange for cremation of the remains within twenty-four hours of the time of death.

Disposition of the ashes has also evolved into a kind of tradition, expressive of the variations in our individual characters. Because he was an ardent angler, Great-grandfather Millis's ashes were transported by train, by Grandfather Carson, to Springfield, in May of 1904. From there they were taken by carriage to the banks of the Connecticut River in Holyoke, there to be scattered on the waters which he'd fished so many times for the large salmon they then held.

Carson's greatest joy, excepting my father, and his work, was sculling on the Charles, and that was where his ashes were strewn. I should mention also that the tradition which calls for disposition of the ashes, also requires that the ceremony be performed at the season which accommodated the decedent's avocation; while January has been the cruelest month for the

Wills men, each of my male forebears dying in the first month of the year, Millis's ashes were retained until the fishing season began in the spring, locked in a vault at the Old Colony Trust Company. Carson's were retained also, until the ice broke and the then-sweet waters were free to carry them to the sea, in 1944. Only the eldest surviving son conducts this one of our customs; the other survivors go about their ordinary business, unaware until after the task has been completed, of the day and hour of its performance.

All of the survivors, though, together with friends of many years, attend the memorial service at Appleton Chapel. That, too, has been ordered by tradition. A summation of his life, a sort of intimate reconciliation of the accounts of friendship and commerce which occupied his hours, a farewell to wife and children, some reflections upon what they and his experiences have meant to him: that consoling catalogue is kept by each of us, starting with the year in which we marry, and revised as events make it appropriate. The firstborn male reads it to the mourners. The pastor then delivers appropriate remarks, commencing with the reading of: "I am the resurrection and the life, saith the Lord: he that believeth in me, though he were dead, yet shall he live." Then whomever the decedent has last designated — in secret, since none of us can know, for whom the bell is destined to toll first, it has often been necessary to solicit the acceptance of a second or third eulogist, the first or second having predeceased a Wills, and to do so without causing the offense of implying that the replacement was not the first choice — from among his friends and colleagues, makes a few brief remarks, and then concludes the service by reading from Tennyson: "Crossing the Bar." For my father, that was Lawrence Barton Cable, the son of my father's first partner, who had died six years before.

It was after Larry had paused, to offer his condolences, and we had been delayed in an aisle of the chapel, Ellen, the boys and I, to receive other expressions of sympathy and admiration for my father, that I emerged from the warmth of the place into the brilliant, cold-sharpened sunlight of the Yard, relieved and yet contented that the ceremonies had been conducted to my father's standard. It was then that the lame man and his companion came up to me. The lame man tapped me on the shoulder with a swagger stick, and further assured my attention by addressing me by name. "Compton," he said, in a husky voice of unusual depth, and I turned.

I had never seen him before. Incorrectly surmising, I think, that I had in some fashion given way to grief, he touched my arm. I have always loathed being touched. "Forgive this intrusion," he said, as I quickly withdrew my arm. "You do not know me, but I knew Cable well, and I shall miss him."

The lame man was about five feet, six inches tall, perhaps seventy years old. His carriage was erect, and he was a burly sort. His face was large, and reddening in the cold. He had a full head of iron-gray hair, cut short to the scalp. He wore a gray suit, waistcoat and lapels visible under his open, dark-gray chesterfield, the ribbon of the Legion of Honor at his lapel.

"I served with him in London," the lame man said. He turned to his companion, a man of about the same age, gaunt, well over six feet, attired in a homburg and a dark-blue overcoat. "Allow me to introduce Landings Jessup." The companion bowed and murmured something that I could not catch, but took to be an offer of condolences, and I accepted it with a bow.

"Many were the nights," the lame man said, "when the three of us were at cards with Cable at White's." Reasonably enough, I think, I glanced around for a third stranger, still without any identification of the first, and very little understanding of what the deuce the second was doing at the chapel either. The lame man saw my perplexity. "Arthur Bayleford," he said, as though that would explain it. "First Sea Lord, in nineteen forty-six. Got a peerage later and called himself Lord Martinsby." Then awareness crept over him.

"I'm terribly sorry," he said, in that compelling voice, "Major General Aubrey T. Gammage, U.S. Army, retired. I met your father in November of 1938, when I was military attaché to the American Embassy to the Court of Saint James's. You had just been born, and as we became friends at once, I heard a great deal about you. He was very proud of you. Very proud. For almost thirty-five years, now, I've been hearing from Cable about how very proud he is of you."

My father died on January twelfth, 1972. He was approaching his seventy-third birthday (March 3, 1899, was his date of birth), and had seemed in good health and spirits when we entertained him at Christmas. Hadley and Lee were his particular pets; he seemed able, with them, to show his affection more openly than he had with me, probably because he did not consider himself obligated to see also to his grandchildren's discipline. That Christmas he allowed himself three whiskies, and a large port after dinner, and to each of the boys gave a check for two hundred dollars for sports equipment. The boys, the previous summer, had become very keen on scuba diving, and intended to acquire air-tanks and suchlike with the funds. To me, Dad gave a Chelsea clock, an object which he himself had long openly coveted for his desk, and I could not resist allowing him for a few minutes to feel self-sacrificing and perhaps just a trifle sorry for himself, until he opened our persent to him, and discovered that it was a Chelsea clock. Then we were all very happy, taking the remainder of the day to catch up with each other on what was doing at the shop (we often remarked how odd it was, that, as he put it, he had achieved his dream of having me in practice with him, close by, and yet found that we were, as he put it, "like ships that pass in the night," never really up-to-date on our conversations). Pleasing him greatly, Ellen openly gloated in the emerald brooch he had given her, and it was early evening before he began to shift around and otherwise hint that he was ready to be driven home to Milton.

In the car, we talked. There was a little snow that year, rather dirty and scant, and as the headlights illumined it along the roadside, he said to me with some sadness: "Can't say's Hester would've been much use this year, even if she hadn't died twelve years ago."

I hadn't thought it was that long.

"Was," he said. "I got up this morning at my usual time," around five-thirty; his physician and his family had long since abandoned the effort to persuade him to get more rest — he said he knew the difference between what was good for him, and what he could do that was good for him, and "lying around in bed all day is one thing that I can't do, too much on my mind and all," and we accepted it as true, "and I was going through my journals again."

Dad, of course, was assuring me that my soliloquy was current and up-to-date, in case it should be needed. "I thought you felt pretty well," I said.

"I do," he said. "I feel first-rate. But a Wills at my age would be a fool if he didn't feel some apprehension as the New Year approaches."

I was silent.

"I saw Andrew in Washington, the end of last week," he said, in his customary, livelier tone.

I was determined to be careful, now. Danielle had been in touch with Ellen, and had conveyed, somewhat hysterically according to Ellen, the fact of their marital difficulties. " 'He's away so much,'" Ellen had quoted her as saying. "She said he suspects her, and accuses her, and she doesn't know what to do. He's told her that he wants a divorce."

So, while I was aware that Dad and Andrew remained close, careful to see each other when their travels intersected, I was not certain that Andrew had seen fit to burden Dad with his troubles. There was, of course, no reason why Andrew should not have made that decision, and quite properly have sought Dad's sage counsel, but it was a decision that I thought best left to Andrew, and I did not intend to usurp it by some unguarded remark.

"I understand that he would be in Las Vegas for the holidays," I said.

"Yes," Dad said. "Awful place, any time of year. Apparently he's gotten some tip about dealing between the President and Howard Hughes.

"*Damn,*" Dad said, agitation noticeable in his voice, using the strongest language that I ever heard him permit himself. "*Damned* if I can fathom that man. I worked the best I could with five Administrations before he came in. Some I agreed with, some I did not, but I worked. The only one I was really comfortable with, philosophically, was Eisenhower's, and I honestly expected better things from this fellow. Better things. Drat that man."

It was best, when he was frustrated, to allow him to work it out, himself. He regarded exasperation as a sign of character defect, and accordingly required no assistance in changing subjects to one which excited him less, and permitted him consequent opportunity to reflect calmly and to speak precisely.

"Andrew's got a new car," Dad said.

"I hadn't heard," I said. I had heard, but I'd seen no reason to inflame Dad needlessly, by telling him. From the time that I was old enough to notice, we had gotten along nicely with a Chevrolet sedan and a Chrysler Newport sedan, both black, each replaced every five years. Dad had had the accountants in the office determine the most favorable period for ownership of a car, given the amount of use we required of it, and they had settled upon that period. I had obtained the same service from them, when Ellen and I moved to Lincoln, and relied upon it then and now: I lease a Plymouth compact for myself, and a Ford compact station wagon for Ellen. Andrew, having made some sort of a killing, had traded a two-year-old Porsche on a new red Jaguar roadster, to Danielle's dismay.

"Devilish damned thing to get in and out of," Dad said. "One of those sports cars. Jaguar, I think."

"Come to think of it," I said, "I guess I had heard. He keeps it in Washington, does he?"

"Yes," Dad said, "he keeps it in Washington." There was a certain grimness in his tone, now. "Matter of fact, well, he didn't tell me this now, and I wouldn't want you to say anything to Ellen . . ."

"I won't," I said.

"Mind, he didn't tell me this, but Andrew's a sort of, well, he's a headstrong young man, very headstrong, and I've lived long enough so that I don't always have to be told something in order to know it, you understand?"

I said: "Yes."

"Well," he said, seemingly satisfied, "I'm not at all sure that the car is the only thing he's keeping in Washington. Keeping company with, at least."

"Oh Jesus," I said.

"Umm," Dad said. "He told me that he and Danielle are probably going to get a divorce."

"Did you talk to him?" I said.

"Talk to him?" Dad said. "Of course I talked to him."

"Because Andrew, as you say, has always been a rather headstrong fellow," I said. "Tendency to go off, half-cocked. I'd hope he wouldn't just decide, some fine morning, to throw away a marriage just because the thought crossed his mind."

"No," Dad said, "I don't think it's that. Not that at all. He demanded confidentiality, and of course I assured him of it, so I'm not at liberty to tell you what he thinks the reasons are that justify his decision. But just like you, that was my first thought, that he was acting rashly. I'm satisfied that he's not."

"He can be self-indulgent," I said.

There was an uncommonly long pause. My father preferred to marshal his thoughts, and to choose carefully the words appropriate to their expression. But this was an unusually long silence. At last he said: "Perhaps he should be. He's fairly sure he won't be paying alimony for long, and perhaps the risk is worth taking."

"How can he be sure of that?" I said. "Danielle's a fine and accomplished woman. But to my understanding, at least, she's never made enough as a ballet dancer to maintain herself in any sort of reasonable comfort. And like the rest of us, she's not getting younger. But it matters more, if you're a dancer, I should think, anyway."

"He believes she's got a boyfriend," Dad said. "If he's right, well, she'll have trouble *getting* much alimony, if any."

"Really?" I said. "Dunnigan handles all of that stuff in the shop, and he doesn't seem to think that's the case anymore."

"It is if the boyfriend's married, and doesn't plan to leave his hearth and home," Dad said. "If he's got any control over her, anyway. Andrew says that he, Andrew, hasn't, but because of that, he's got nothing to lose."

"Can he prove it?" I said. "In court, I mean."

"Said he can't, yet," Dad said, "but she doesn't know that." He sighed. "I don't know. He could be lying to me, trying to make me feel better. People do that to you, when they think you're getting old and they don't want to upset you. So, when they've decided to do something, well, perhaps you're right. Maybe he's just being self-indulgent, and making up something about her that he thinks'll make it all right with me. And perhaps that's what he should be doing. Whatever he wants."

"Really?" I said.

There was fatigue and uncertainty in his voice now, almost palpable, as we swung smoothly off Route 128, onto Randolph Avenue, almost home.

"I'm not as sure of things as I used to be," he said in the darkness, only the lights of the dash to cast a pale green light on his features when I sneaked a look at him. "Who am I to condemn him? We all do it. I've done it."

"You've concealed it from me, then," I said.

"You just haven't noticed it," he said. We had turned off Randolph Avenue, made the requisite turns, and now approached the main house on the hill, its lights welcoming us. I turned in at the drive. Somewhat sourly, he said: "Let me not to the marriage of true minds admit impediments, but does that tell you anything?"

It did, of course. My mother died in 1954, in May, while I was at Exeter. Afflicted with what at first seemed nothing more than a bad chest cold, she progressed into racking spells of coughing that drove her to her bed, and at last to summon a physician. He found bronchial pneumonia, probably brought on by her insistence upon not only supervising the gardeners, but getting down on her knees on the wet turf with them, early in April, before it was warm enough to work outdoors, fussing over her tulips and crocuses before the last snow was gone from the flowerbeds. He prescribed bed rest, and certain antibiotics. The day after I received this news, by telephone at school, I was informed by the headmaster that she had suffered a pulmonary embolism in her sleep.

Dad kept the house. "I never really ever considered getting

rid of it," he said, as we drove toward it on that Christmas night. "Oh, I considered it. And while I knew what I should do, I put it off. I used you as an excuse, I used Andrew as an excuse — he had no other place to go, if I closed the house and dismissed Betsey, and neither did she, although she wasn't really needed anymore, with you away at school all winter, and the summer too. But I justified it. You can always justify doing what you want to do. What I was doing was important, and it demanded that I travel, winter and summer both, without regard to your needs or vacations, and I decided to keep this place, which I really didn't need, to give you boys a home base until you had grown.

"That," he said, "was more than seventeen years ago. Somewhere along the line, what was mostly my selfishness became entirely my selfishness." As I pulled up to the door and began to get out of the car, he turned to me. "Don't," he said. "If I have to have a house of this size, I'm still spry enough to get out of a car and open a door by myself. Merry Christmas, Comp, and Godspeed."

That was not the last time that I saw him alive. I saw him on Monday, the twenty-seventh, at the office, and we chatted briefly. He seemed to be in good shape, and we made plans for lunch at the Union Club, for the twenty-eighth. He expressed surprise, recalling that I had told him I would have to miss our usual Tuesday because I would be out of town.

"Ted Fullerton called from the Creighton Labs, New York office," I said. "Told me he's been catching hell from his wife and his doctor and everybody else at the company about working too hard. He's getting out of town. Won't be back for a week. I've canceled at the Gotham." Dad seemed pleased.

Nevertheless, we missed that Tuesday lunch. On the afternoon of the twenty-seventh, he received a telephone call that took him to Washington for three days. I saw him on Friday, but he had a number of people in his office, and we had no chance to talk. That weekend was New Year's Eve, which Ellen and I traditionally spent with the Fields, and Dad preferred to be left alone on New Year's. He said he did, at least, and I obeyed his wishes. On the third I went straight from home to the airport, for a business meeting in St. Louis. I did not return until Friday, the seventh, and learned that Dad had gone back to Washington, expecting to return the following Monday night, the tenth. I reserved our usual table for the eleventh, but he was delayed, and did not return until evening.

On the morning of the twelfth, he was in high spirits. I must note, here, that he was never less than genuinely regretful of his obligation to keep confidential the business that he conducted for his clients. But he carried their attorney-client privilege to what seemed to me to be extreme lengths, often refusing to disclose so much as their identities. Since it obviously pained him to deny you an answer to your question, one learned early never to inquire, and thus to spare him the necessity of declining to divulge what he felt he must keep secret. We decided to meet for lunch on the thirteenth, but on the afternoon of the twelfth he received an urgent summons to return to Washington, paused by the door of my office, his face alight, and said he would see me on Friday.

That night, in his bed at the Hay-Adams Hotel, Daniel Cable Wills died in his sleep.

Outside the chapel, General Gammage and Landings Jessup seemed reluctant to permit me to escape with my family and my friends. All were cold, as was I, and yet I could not be so rude as to walk away from him. Andrew lurked in the foyer, talking to Ellen, out of earshot.

"In these times," Gammage said, "he was a very unusual man."

Respectfully, I said: "He was an unusual man in any times."

Jessup started to say something, but deferred to Gammage. Gammage spoke urgently in that husky voice. It seemed obvious he would keep me there until he finished. "Ah, young man," he said, poking me in the chest with his right forefinger, glancing every so often to Jessup, for confirmation and receiving it by signals of vigorous nods, "but he was a *patriot*. A patriot of the kind that this university used to provide to the country as a matter of *course*. Cable Wills loved his country. He loved it. He *sacrificed* for it." He poked me again. "Remember that, my boy, remember it. It will console you."

I soon discovered extremely good reason to remember it. The only deficiency in General Gammage's assessment was its lack of detail, and that, I am sorry to say, was soon repaired. That night, two years ago, as we proceeded into the Hole, Andrew began that repair. "The lame man," he said, "was an out-and-out spy, for Wild Bill Donovan in the OSS. And Daniel Cable Wills was his contact man."

I was astonished. I was absolutely astonished. In the darkness I said: "Andrew, have you, at long last, lost your mind?"

V

My mother's death, partly because I was so unprepared for it, partly because I was not yet sixteen years old, utterly devastated me. She had been in my life the sole source of tenderness, solicitude, warmth and affection. She had been my confidante in everything but those genital subjects which I learned about from my chums at school, and a good deal of what I learned from them, I might add, was wrong. Until the night, three years later, when as a member of Porcellian I had been invited to the stag line at a gathering on Beacon Hill, and met Ellen Shipp Hadley, I was thoroughly lost.

I can recall that evening well. Formally attired, we arrived at the townhouse on Mount Vernon Street near the top of the Hill. We entered, the six of us, through the wrought-iron gate in the fence, and started up the walk. In the tall windows of the house, lights blazed, and although it only just then stopped snowing, one of the windows had been opened slightly. Behind the window was the Hadleys' Steinway. Seated at it was a thin young man, then, I later learned, deemed Ellen's best beau. The gaslights on the Hill shone yellow on the snow, and from the music room came the "Moonlight" Sonata. We wore long white silk scarves in those days, and flung them over our shoulders as we approached the door. Inside, where the fire burned brightly in the grate, she was presented to me, all in white, with a white ribbon in her hair, and what I had considered myself to feel for Patience Judith Hood of Cohasset, then a rather severe student of Romance languages at Radcliffe, I immediately forgot.

Less expeditious, I regret to say, was my recovery from the death of my father, a fact which is equaled in distress for me only by the astonishment which accompanies the dismay. I was, after all, a man of maturity when he died. I was married, and held a respected position in the community. I was prepared for my responsibilities, because he had seen to that, and I carried them out, I think, with fair success.

I am sorry to say that I was unable to do so with even that melancholy satisfaction that would normally attend the discharge of a sacred duty, however mournful. On June the first, as he had directed, of 1972, I informed my secretary — an excellent woman, Rachel, who demanded to work for me when my father died, after twenty-three years as his secretary, advising me that this had been his wish — that I would be absent from the office, on personal business, on the second. The next morning, while it was still dark, I left Ellen sleeping peacefully in our bed, dressed, and very early in the day boarded the *Nobska* at Woods Hole. I carried a small shopping bag from S. S. Pierce. It contained a one-half-gallon ice cream carton, the lid secured with a length of masking tape. The vessel made steam.

In the full sunlight of that Friday, as we approached N26 off Nantucket, I obeyed my instructions, went aft and removed the carton from the bag. Using the knife which I had brought, I slit the tape. I waited, watching the gulls wheel in the air around the old steamer, until we were entering the harbor at N11, the black can to port at Brant Point Light, I removed the lid and saw inside the gray ashes and shell-like chips of white bone that had survived the fire. I poured them into the water where the tourists, departing from the island, hurl their pennies, in order to assure that they will soon return to Nantucket. For Cable Wills, the books were closed. To the island to which he had fled, in 1961, when to him it seemed that newcomers to Duxbury required his own immediate departure, he had now, for the last time, returned. The gulls swept in over the surface where I'd strewn him, saw nothing for themselves, and rose away again. I put the shopping bag in the trashcan.

I must begin with events that occurred before I was born, and I do so with all the trepidation of any lawyer with nothing to rely upon but fragmentary hearsay. I believe this was the way that matters developed, and that is all that I can say.

My great-grandfather, Millis Wills, was the son of a minister who is said to have been acquainted with John Quincy Adams. He obtained a living from a parish in Dedham. He was married to a woman named Judith Hope Millis. That is contained on the first page of my father's journal, evidently copied from the first page of my grandfather's journal, which also records the birth of Judith Millis Wills, three years later, in 1827. In my grandfather's journal, after her name, there is this notation: "D.?"

Millis Wills, after graduation from the College, settled in Plymouth. I am sorry to admit that I never inquired about his business there, but I seem to recall that he was at first in the shipbuilding trade. He married Dorothea Prudence Carson. Apparently he was excused from service with the Union Army, or else procured a substitute. In 1863, the year after his son, Carson, was born, he moved to Duxbury. That same year, another son, Donald, was born. Millis died on January third, 1867; Carson's journal records that fact, with the notation that it was "consumption" which carried him off (probably cancer; sixty was a pretty good age for a man in those times). Carson's journal also records that Donald Carson Wills was reported lost at sea on January 7, 1879, when the vessel of which he was first mate, proceeding from Plymouth to Marblehead, was overdue. If his body was ever found, it is not noted.

Carson, '81, was silent about his activities immediately after college. But by 1894, he was engaged in the solo practice of law, in Boston. I have determined that from records of the firm, to which I might usefully have paid closer attention some time ago.

Those records show that Carson Wills and Theodore Michael Harper executed articles of partnership for the practice of law, with offices at 14 Beacon Street, Boston, on January first, 1895. There are extant no originals or copies of the contract partnership, which entirely comports with the long-standing refusal of lawyers, ever insistent upon agreements in writing for their clients, of manifesting similar prudence in the conduct of their own affairs. My father was uncommonly conscientious: he actually had a will, and it had been kept up to date, revised and with several codicils added after my mother's death, acknowledged by the requisite number of witnesses, and kept in a safe place. Very unusual for a lawyer, making sure that his own estate was in order. I did not fully approve of

the instructions which it gave me, as coexecuter with the Old
Colony Trust Company, but it was clear, and if it induced
puzzlement, in its distributions, at least my chores in making
them were plainly stated.

Apparently the partnership of Wills & Harper failed to prosper as the venturers had hoped. The records of the firm show
that Carson Wills conducted four trials in the Suffolk Superior
Court during 1895, and billed his clients somewhere in the
neighborhood of a total of $2,150, $1,850 of which the firm
appears to have collected. The files also show that Harper, at
the end of 1895, received a letter from what seems to have
been his principal client, reporting that the success of a com-
peting product, Lydia E. Pinkham's Vegetable Compound,
had obliterated his market and left him without resources to
compensate Mr. Harper for his very valuable assistance and
legal services. Mr. Harper's reply, if he reduced one to writing,
is not recorded.

Harper vanishes without a trace from the firm records, after
that. Carson Wills did not see fit to include a memorandum to
file on that event, and if Harper did, it is not extant. But on
July 3, 1896, there was dispatched a letter over the signature of
Lawrence Harrison Cable, informing one James J. Marshall
that Daniel Carson Wills and Lawrence Harrison Cable, Es-
quires, will be pleased to see to his representation in a certain
controversy, concerning a will, in the Probate Court for the
County of Norfolk, upon the 18th, inst.

If the partial records still remaining are any indication,
Lawrence Harrison Cable and Carson Wills formed a team of
extraordinary felicity. The more felicitous because, as Carson's
journal records, on May 15, 1897, he was joined in wedlock
with Anne Dussault Cable, in a ceremony performed at Appleton Chapel. He was thirty-five years old.

About a year before my father was born, the firm of Wills &

Cable was pleased to announce that Thomas James Marshall had been admitted to the firm as a partner, the firm to be known as Wills, Cable & Marshall. There followed, between 1898 and 1899, several pieces of correspondence indicating that as many as fifteen associates (as they now would be called) were brought in as clerks, observed, in some instances kept on and in some, let go. As the firm entered the twentieth century, as nearly as I can determine, there were three full partners — Carson Wills, L. H. Cable, and T. J. Marshall (who may have been related to James J. Marshall — each had a Topsfield address — but I cannot be sure). There may have been one more: a John Albert Hammond (he signed his first name: *Jno.*) appears on some of the correspondence, and writes very authoritatively, but his tenure seems to have begun sometime in 1903, and he does not appear after 1906.

Something extraordinary happened early in 1907. I can imagine the excitement that must have filled the offices of Wills, Cable & Marshall on the seventh floor at 14 Beacon, where the best offices looked out over the Old Granary Burial Ground, the graves of Sam Adams and the other patriots. My grandfather took me there often, and so did my father, when I was a child, riding up in the elevator enclosed in the wrought-iron shaft, walking proudly across the marble floors into the bustling office. Oh, they would have been restrained, it is true, no breaking out of bottles or suchlike, but surely there must have been some celebration when the first of four coveted clients came to the firm, and then mounting exultation as the next three followed, and what had been a touch-and-go operation was suddenly established, and seemingly permanent. The difficulty is that I cannot determine which of the clients was first. That was the day that they must have exulted. But before the year was out, the files were fat with correspondence dealing with the interests of the Plymouth & Brockton Street Railway Co., the Boston Elevated Railway Co., the Standard Oil Company (seeking regional representation), and what may perhaps have seemed, then, to be the least but surely nevertheless desirable client, the New England Manufacturers Bank, newly established in offices at 73 Tremont Street.

Those were tributes to skill, and the skill which they acknowledged was principally that of Carson Wills. By that I do not mean to take away a single iota of credit from Lawrence Harrison Cable, to whom my grandfather, Carson, extended in my presence the full respect that he accorded only to equals.

"Harrison Cable," as my father never hesitated to inform me, "got the business. Dad," he meant: my grandfather, "was certainly one of the most formidable trial counsel in Massachusetts in those days. As good as Choate, as good as any of them. In his heyday, he was as good as anybody in the country. But it was Harrison Cable who got the business, and Tom Marshall who kept after it. What they used Dad" (Granddad) "for was to make sure that anyone who wanted to make trouble, got much more trouble than he wanted. And Dad always delivered.

"It was a victorious combination: Harrison could get it; Tom could keep it, always reassuring the clients that Dad would protect them in court, if they didn't get what they wanted, outside; and then Dad would go into court when that happened, and get it. Dad was the last resort, but he was always the best one. He kept the opposition honest."

That may have been the reason for the facts that I uncovered, once I started looking. Granddad, when Dad entered the firm, in 1920, was only fifty-eight years old. When I was born, eighteen years later, there was still sufficient time yet remaining to him, for me to get to know him in the fullness of his powers.

My father must have chafed at that. He was a man who occupied a room, when he entered it. But when he entered

Wills, Cable & Marshall, on that July morning more than fifty years ago, it was already occupied. By Carson. I believe Cable Wills, on that day or soon after, began to look elsewhere. But I cannot be sure, to this day, that Andrew Collier was correct in his speculation. And I insist it was no more than that.

VI

WE HAD the Nobska Light to temper the deepening evening now, and the seas were running lower, around two feet. Andrew at the wheel had us well on course to enter the Hole as the current set to the east at one and a quarter knots, not quite as good as slack water, but entirely satisfactory.

"The trouble with Priddy," he said, "is that he wants you to give him the whole story before he's willing, really willing, to okay the money you need to go and get the whole story.

"Now," he said, "I haven't *got* the whole story. I'm not even sure I can get the whole story, or that anybody else can, either. I had to explain all that to him, slowly and painfully, which I wouldn't think oughta be necessary with a guy who's been a bureau chief for as long as he has, but apparently it is.

"This whole thing started," he said, "oh, three or four years ago. Well, it *started* years and years ago, I think, but I didn't know anything about it, or start to get onto it, until I started hearing things from the Humphrey people in nineteen sixty-eight. Nothing I could print, just things that I heard.

"I didn't get anywhere, chasing those leads down," Andrew said, stretching and shifting position at the wheel. "I didn't get anywhere in nineteen seventy-two, either, working the same turf again. I sure as God should have, but I didn't. What I did get, by accident, was a tip I should have run down, but ignored because it didn't seem very important and because it wasn't a good story I was after, it was Nixon. So, when I got this anonymous call about something funny going on with bonds that were supposedly being issued by some bank on one of the Channel Islands, I didn't pay any attention to it. I had other things on my mind.

"Then, about the middle of July, when just about one more story about Henry Kissinger and the CIA would've made me vomit if I knew what it was when it came to me, I got a call from a man I swore I'd never identify, so I won't. But I've had conversations with this gentleman in the past, and I have strong reason to believe that he's a member in good standing of a certain honored society. Maybe several of 'em, in fact, now that I think of it.

"Now this guy is not young, like you and me, Dan," and Deirdre laughed in that silvery way that she has, as did Andrew, "and he has been around for a very long time and knows a great many people. And everything he ever told me, that I could check, he was right about. So, when he calls me up, I tend to listen, attentively, and to go and meet him at the time and place he selects. It's harder now than it used to be, since

I've become a star of stage and screen and busybodies can recognize me more easily and start to wonder what the hell a guy's doing talking to me when the people he hangs around with don't want him talking to people like me, but we manage. If you can call meeting in a fourth-floor room at the Hotel McAlpin *managing*. What he told me, in about twelve minutes — he doesn't like to spend any more time on a thing'n he has to — was that somebody in the Bahamas was doing something with counterfeit bonds of the Bank of Sark, and skinning a lot of millionaires with them. American millionaires, who couldn't complain because then the IRS'd start snooping around to see if they paid the taxes on those millions they had salted away in Bahamian banks.

"July, he tells me this," Andrew said. " 'You couldn't've called me in February, of course, when I could use a trip to the West Indies?' No, he could not. This guy never explains anything, why he decides to tell me something, or why he decides at a particular time. And I do not ask. I think his motives are probably dishonorable, depending on your point of view, but he can square himself with his Maker when the time comes, and I'll get my own girl. Are you sure I can't have a bourbon, Deirdre? I've been an awful good boy by anybody's standards."

She got up, saying: "All right. But just one."

"Good," he said. "Night vision, you know. Jim Beam's very good for night vision."

She went below.

"Now I am not dumb," Andrew said. "A little slow on the uptake sometimes, maybe, but not dumb. It was gonna take a hell of a lot more than the results of ten or twelve minutes in a room at the McAlpin to get a trip to Nassau out of Priddy, even in the off-season when all the schoolteachers go, and make your life miserable going around chattering like magpies. So I started doing some digging, kind of bored, really, but having nothing better to do, and at first I got nowhere at a very great rate."

Deirdre came up the companionway and handed him a glass with ice and bourbon in it. He drank from it and said what he always says: "Ah, good. This's hot work. Makes a man thirsty.

"Then," he said, "Priddy interrupted my meditations with a strong suggestion that I should maybe devote some time to a story that the paper could possibly print before we were all eligible for retirement, and he sent me down to Morgantown, West Virginia, to talk to a fellow from the UMW about what effect it'd have on the miners' eligibility rules if all the utility companies switched from oil back to coal for their boilers. We'd already had a story out of New York about that, that Senator Tobin was all hot to trot for the idea, and if there's one thing that pisses Priddy off, it's New York getting a story, as he puts it, 'that we should've had if one of you bastards'd only get off your goddamned ass and go up on the Hill and start asking people some fucking questions.' So he plays catch-up ball, and we get to do the work.

"Well, I went down there," Andrew said. "Nothing like scenic Morgantown, around the first of August when any sensible person with an independent means of income" — my father had left ten thousand dollars to Andrew, *in trust nevertheless*, so that all he would get until he retired, *or at age sixty-five, whichever shall sooner occur*, was the income. It came to about a thousand dollars a year — "would haul ass for Nantucket on the first available plane.

"Now I have been in Morgantown before," Andrew said. "I was in Morgantown in nineteen sixty, when JFK was dashing about, so I know before I get there that they have a restaurant in those parts which serves the very worst pizza in the world, bar none, hands down. You can't fool me, boy; I remember things." In the twilight now, he tapped his forehead.

"I have also been down in the mines. I have been in the changing rooms and the shower rooms, where those poor bastards can scrub another shift after they come to the surface from the working shift, and still not get the stuff off.

"Jesus, Deirdre," he said, "you oughta see those guys. They have got to be the toughest men in the world. They've each got a metal basket, looks like it's made of heavy-duty screening, like a grocery cart, and it's hitched to this chain that goes over a pulley at the rafters and comes down to a cleat on a post, and they lock it. With a padlock. When they come to work, they unlock the thing and lower the basket down, and take their working clothes out of it, undress, put their street clothes and valuables in the basket, hoist it back up to the rafters, and get ready to go down into the mine. Every single one of them's a fatalist, I swear. There're these signs on the walls, reminding them not to spit in the corners because it's dangerous and unsanitary. Now think about that for a minute: why is it dangerous and unsanitary? Well, for one thing, it's because the phlegm they cough up has probably got black lung infectants in it, and the owners don't want the ones that haven't got it yet, getting it from the ones that have. Just stalling off death a little longer, is all they're accomplishing."

"I shouldn't think the ones that haven't got it yet would mind, though," Deirdre said.

"They don't mind," Andrew said. "They really don't mind. The owners provide masks for them, so they won't inhale the dust, or as much of it, anyway, and I bet no more'n ten percent of them use them. You can spot the ones that do: washed or unwashed, they've got white muzzles, where the masks stop the dust from getting into the pores. I asked one of the other guys why he didn't use one, and this was a fairly young man, too. He said: 'Look, I'm not gonna live long enough, to die from the lung. If I don't touch an open circuit' — the power systems for the lights and drills down there'd scare the shit out of you just to look at them — 'then it'll be a cave-in, or a blast.' There's a lot more explosions of that dust'n you ever hear about up here.

"Anyway," Andrew said, "I wasn't getting much of anywhere with the people I was talking to. If they'd thought about the possibilities of more business at all, they hadn't thought about them much, and they said just about what you'd've expected them to say. Strictly ho-hum, and then I ran into the Reverend Angus Llewellyn.

"I met the Reverend in nineteen sixty," Andrew said. "He's one of the goddamnedest human beings I have ever seen in my life. He's about six-four, and he must weigh at least two hundred and forty pounds, not an ounce of it fat. He's one of six brothers, and every one of the others is a minister, too. Church of the Full Gospel. If there's something you want to get done in West Virginia, and you've got to persuade the miners to go along with it, get in touch with Angus Llewellyn or one of his brothers, talk them into it, and be patient.

"The Kennedys knew that. The Kennedys knew everything. At least they knew more'n Nixon and had the decent dignity to stick to screwing, and leave the thieving go. So they were very polite to the Reverend Angus, and there was this night when JFK couldn't keep a scheduled appearance 'way up in the hills with the Reverend, where the men who worked in Cherokee Number Four lived. So they substituted Ted.

"I was as new as he was, then," Andrew said. "Each of us got a lot of compliments about our energy and enthusiasm, which was for him a genuine piece of praise, and for me a reminder that certain people were jealous of me, and did not think I had enough experience. Which, at the time, was true, because what if some son of a bitch'd picked that night to take a shot at JFK, while I was riding around in the woods with Teddy and the Reverend? But they didn't.

"The Reverend showed up, expecting to collect Jack. Looked just like Wyatt Earp. Black suit, black string tie, black hat, black boots. No revolvers, but otherwise, Wyatt Earp the way you always dreamed he looked and certainly never did. Took the bad news very well. Off we went, me, him and Teddy, into the dark. And when I say *dark*, I mean dark; they may dig the coal to make the steam to generate the electricity what keeps de cities bright, down there, but they don't waste no hard-earned profits on lights for those mountain roads. If the stars ain't enough for you, Joxer, well, tough shit.

"Seemed like we rode for hours. The Reverend's not a talkative sort, and I didn't have a whole lot of advice to the fellow that was with me about how to make a name for himself in this world, so it was dark and quiet and, really, kind of ominous.

"Finally we got to this church, away the hell and gone out in the wilderness, one of the churches that the Reverend served, he had about twelve of them, I guess, and we went inside. We were late, and we didn't have the guy they expected to hear. Must've been three hundred of them in there, sitting on folding chairs, looking like they took the night off from living in hell just to listen to this rich kid that wanted to be President of the United States, and now they weren't even gonna get him, but his kid brother.

"Those churches are not what you'd call elaborate. There was a platform up at the front, and there was a long table and some chairs, and the Reverend insisted there had to be another one, and I had to sit in it, because I was from the *New York Times*. There was no way in the world I was telling that man anything in the world. If the Reverend Angus wanted to think I was from the *Times*, then by Jesus I was from the *Times*.

Any way he wanted it, in that group. We sat down and the Reverend stood up, and all those hard guys sat there looking like kids waiting for the Punch and Judy show to start.

"The Reverend reaches under the table and he brings up a lectern. Makes a few preliminary remarks, calling down the blessings of God on his assemblage. He was about twenty-five years old, I guess, no more'n that, and all those hardbitten bastards bowed their heads and said 'Amen' when he told them so, like he was the Prophet Isaiah himself.

"Then he reached into the lectern," Andrew said, "and he pulls out this folded flag, and he shook it out and held it up. 'This,' he said, 'is the flag of the greatest country in the world.' They seemed to like that. They all nodded. No dispute about that. 'This is the flag that flew over Valley Forge,' which wasn't strictly true, but we made no disagreements, 'and Gettysburg and over Belleau Wood. It went onto the beaches at Normandy, and the shores of Guadalcanal, and it flew proudly on Mount Suribachi, at Iwo Jima. This is the same flag that flew from PT One-Oh-Nine.' There was a general murmur of approval. Sounded like a pride of contented lions. 'I'm gonna take this flag,' the Reverend said, 'and I'm gonna put it here on this table, because this is the flag with the blue of the skies of West Virginia, and the white of American purity, and the red of the blood of her patriots.' And he did it.

" 'Now,' says the Reverend, and he reaches under the lectern again, 'I hold here in my hand the Holy Bible. In this book is contained all the wisdom and truth of the Prophets, and the writings of the wise men, and of Jesus Christ, the Son of God.' Several of them said 'Amen.'

" 'I am gonna take this Holy Bible,' says the Reverend, 'containin' all the truth and wisdom that the world has ever known, and I'm gonna place it here upon this flag, which has the blue of the skies over West Virginia, and the white of the purity of our American purpose, and the red of the blood of the patriots shed for our liberty.' And he did it.

" 'Now,' says the Reverend, reaching again, and that whole church was totally, completely silent, 'I show you this candle.' And he held up about a ten-inch white candle in a brass holder just like that little kid in the Doctor Dentons used to have in the Fisk Tire ads, and when he did it, somebody that neither one of us'd noticed hit the main switch, and every light in the hall went out. *Bang.* Total darkness.

" 'This candle,' says the Reverend, 'is the symbol of light, and intelligence, and learning, and of faith.' We could hear him striking a wooden match on the side of the lectern. Honest to God, when that match lighted, it seemed to be as big as a torch. 'I'm gonna light this candle,' he said, and he did it. 'I'm gonna take this candle,' and you oughta see three hundred or so faces black with coal dust, staring at you in the light of one candle, 'and I am gonna place this symbol of our faith in *God* on His Book, which contains all His wisdom and truth, and on that flag with the blue of the West Virginia skies, the white of American purity, the red of her patriots' blood and stars of God's heaven.' And he did it.

"Then he said," Andrew said, "and his voice dropped then. Very loud to very soft, still no lights on, just that one single candle burning 'Tonight we've got a man to speak to us, the brother of the man who represents that liberty and freedom of this flag, the wisdom and the truth of that Holy *Bible*, and the faith that we mean by that candle, the next President of the United States, John F. Kennedy!'

"They came out of their seats like they'd been launched," Andrew said. "The lions weren't contented any longer. If Richard M. Nixon'd been within a mile in the dark, if Hubert Horatio Humphrey or Adlai E. Stevenson'd been reckless enough to come into that hall that night, they'd've been torn limb from limb. Cheering? Holy Jesus, did they cheer, and as Teddy stood up, he leaned over to me and whispered: 'To follow that act, I'm gonna have to commit suicide.'

"Well," Andrew said, as we veered off Nobska Point in the gathering darkness, the only light on our faces the red from the lamps of the instruments, the wind of the evening cool on our faces, "that was the night I knew it didn't matter if Franklin Delano Roosevelt, Junior, made nasty remarks about Humphrey's war record, because John F. Kennedy was gonna carry West Virginia if the Reverend Angus Llewellyn had anything to say about it, and he surely did. But it was also the night, after Teddy made a damned good speech that didn't come close to what the Reverend'd done, and didn't need to, after what the Reverend'd done and we were going back down those terrible mountain roads, that I heard something that I didn't remember until I saw the Reverend again this summer.

"We were all wrung out," Andrew said. "It was close to midnight, and while it may be possible that the flame of that one small candle could truly light the *world*, it did not make up for the lack of sleep that got you when you started at five o'clock in the morning and didn't quit 'til after midnight, day after day after day. So I wasn't paying much attention when Teddy, always looking to learn something, asked the Reverend some question, and the Reverend said: 'The nominal owner is the Rachel Fletcher Paint Company. Supposedly they use coal by-products to make plastics, in one of their subsidiaries. They're exploiters, there's no question about that. But nobody seems to be able to find out who they are, what interests, what people, own the Rachel Fletcher Paint Company. All we get down here is a lot of people in blue suits who look just like each other, and never say very much at all, except to say that we ought to reduce our questions to writing, and forward them to the regional offices in Philadelphia.'

"Now keep in mind," Andrew said, "that when I ran into the Reverend Angus at the end of July, it was not because I looked him up, renewing old acquaintances and all of that. It was strictly accidental. I stopped in a place for a cup of coffee in Morgantown after some twerp on the faculty at West Virginia University'd just given me one and one-half hours of totally useless guff about coal utilization, and all I wanted was time enough to sit by myself and try to think of something I could write about the area that'd constitute a story good enough to get Priddy off my back for long enough to let me dig into the Bank of Sark story, and maybe get enough to get him to let me go ahead with it. But I ran into the Reverend, and in trying to think of something else besides Lee Harvey Oswald to talk about, just sort of idly asked him how the owners were behaving, fifteen years later. I was still working on the coal story.

" 'About the same,' he said. 'Well, a little better. You see, they think now there's a chance they may be able to make a lot of money for themselves, by destroying the countryside, so they're a little more careful of the men who'll have to do the destruction for them, because they need to make a living.'

" 'Did you ever find out who they are?' I said.

" 'Yes,' said the Reverend. 'Well, one of them, at least. We have the identity of one of them. One of the people involved with the Rachel Fletcher Paint Company is a man named Henry Morgan.'

"Now I was still in the dark," Andrew said. "Well, I recognized the name of Henry Morgan, of course, and I knew what that meant. But all it meant to me was that maybe I was part of the way to a story on coal that'd get Priddy off of my back, because anything that's got Henry Morgan in it, is a built-in story."

"I thought he was dead," I said.

"I didn't know he was alive," Deirdre said. "I never heard of the guy."

"That's because you don't hang around in low-class joints and dens of iniquity, my sheltered precious," Andrew said. "Or in high-class law firms, for that matter. Henry Morgan, given his history, appears to have eschewed the methods of his namesake only because he found them coarse. Or unproductive. After all, why go around waving a cutlass and getting your eye put out so you have to wear a patch over it, if you can do the same thing, much more profitably, with a few cooperative bankers, a ballpoint pen, and an Air Travel credit card, while at the same time enjoying comparative comfort in the Bahamas? Henry Morgan is a pirate, in a raw silk suit and Johnston and Murphy shoes and a Corum gold coin watch, perhaps, but a pirate nonetheless. He's old, now. He must be at least eighty-five. But he's been on the fringes of every single major scam, swindle, flimflam and con game attempted in this world since he came into it. And he's never gotten caught."

Andrew looked at me. In the dim light from the instruments, I am glad to say, he could not see my face. I knew what he was about to do, and I hated him for it.

"Lemme put it this way, darlin'," Andrew said. "You've heard of Albert Fall, correct?"

"Of course," she said.

"Okay," Andrew said. "Henry Morgan probably's never been within six hundred miles of Casper, Wyoming, or even somewhere west of Laramie, for that matter, where there's a girl who loves the blend of the wild and the tame. And there's another thing that Mister Fall might well have envied Mr. Morgan, when he got himself indicted for fooling around with the naval oil reserves at the Teapot Dome: if my sources are any good, and they are, I insist, fucking *excellent*, Morgan was one of the principal cats that put Fall up to it."

"Goodness," Ellen said.

"More to come, as we say," Andrew said. He looked at me again. I said nothing, but I could cheerfully have strangled him. He looked back at the women. I saw his head move. "Henry Morgan was Daniel Cable Wills' client."

VII

ELLEN IS a wonderful woman. She is of even temperament, trained intelligence (she prepared at Beaver for Wellesley) and generous spirit (she was very active in the civil rights marches of the middle 1960s, and when Larry Cable and Dad expressed their reservations about her dedication, I was quick to assert my full support for her commitment). But she has never accepted the essential premise that a law firm cannot function if it vets its clients on ideological grounds, and agrees to represent only those with whom its lawyers are in full personal sympathy.

We represent Creighton Labs, for example, a small industrial chemical research firm established in the late 1960s by several scientists theretofore employed by Dow Chemical, but desirous of managing their own fortunes. One of them was my classmate Ted Fullerton, with whom I lived at Eliot House. Fine fellow, Ted. A good friend. I handled their incorporation and profit-sharing matters, while Torbert Kenney of our firm advised them on tax matters. When they went public, for additional capital, in 1970, I represented them before the Securities and Exchange Commission. Dad did what was necessary for them in Great Britain and the Common Market countries. For a small firm, begun almost entirely with borrowed money, the founding venturers have with our help built a company with gross sales in excess of three million dollars a year, returning substantial rewards to themselves and their employees, repaying debts promptly, and never missing a quarterly dividend since going public.

Their work with congeners, esters, and certain binders which revolutionized manufacturing methods involving resins, is well known and respected throughout the world. In these parlous times, economically, they maintain a payroll of more than one hundred and twenty people, and branch offices in New York, Palo Alto and Spokane, managed from the main plant in Burlington. Our annual retainer from Creighton is in the medium of five figures, and our annual settlement billing generally exceeds that.

Inasmuch as I developed the client, the bulk of that fee is credited to me in the partnership ledgers, an important consideration which I have never, in this connection, been able adequately to explain to Ellen. She is convinced that partners are people who share equally in whatever money there is to be shared. Ellen's father, the pastor of the All Saints Church in Concord, had a small competence of his own, and a regular salary; never rich, she was never insecure, either, and has no direct experience whatsoever of the anxiety which the independent entrepreneur experiences daily, calculating whether income in a given year will exceed expenses, and if so, whether by a comfortable sum.

Soon after Dad died, in 1972, the Students for a Democratic Society discovered that Creighton's three-million-dollar annual business included, for 1971 and 1972, a subcontract with MIT, let for assistance and performance of an MIT contract with the Department of Defense, and calling for certain pure research which, if successful, might be applied to the modification of production of military defoliants. It was all very speculative. There was an equally good prospect that the substances under study might prove to have no military use at all, but could be produced cheaply enough and in sufficient quantities to be used on such applications as the median strips of interstate highways, retarding the growth of vegetation without destroying it, and thus preserving necessary antierosion measures while at the same time eliminating the substantial expenses of mowing land abutting pavements.

Scorning such distinctions in their zeal to make needless trouble, the SDS publicized only the potential application of Creighton's work to the conflict in Viet Nam. There was an immediate response from various ecology groups, which in my experience have been at least as excitable as the radical students, though of course much better behaved in the demonstration of their agitation, and none of them approved of Creighton's work.

While I cannot be sure, I think it likely that Ellen is a member of every such existing group. I am certain that she belongs to every one that ever obtained her name from a mailing list. She has dispatched my hard-earned dollars to the protection of whales, the salvation of alligators, the rescue of wildlife threatened with drowning by African hydroelectrical projects, and the dissuasion of people who make their livings by clubbing baby seals to death in the Arctic Archipelago. The energies and emotions which she spent upon the Southern Christian Leadership Conference, the NAACP, and the Student Nonviolent Coordinating Committee, ten years ago, she now exhausts in protests of species endangered by anything other than four-legged predators, a diversion so far preferable to what intervened — opposition to the war in Viet Nam — that I accept it with what I think to be excellent grace.

Unfortunately for me, the ecology groups did not coordinate the cries of alarm which they uttered about Creighton's subcontract. Rather, they reacted serially, and consequently Ellen was not merely cross for one night, but quarrelsome for about two weeks, as one after another checked in with the news about Creighton.

"How can you represent them?" she would demand, as we had what was supposed to be a drink to relax before dinner. And as patiently as I could, I would recite the obligation of the attorney to undertake all ethical and legal tasks required by a client who comes to him in exercise of his constitutional right and good judgment to have the assistance of counsel.

"You don't take other criminal cases," she said. "The firm doesn't represent just people who commit crimes; you've said so yourself."

Soon after I entered practice, Ellen's best friend from college, in anger at what I take to have been a hasty and unhappy marriage, became intoxicated one evening, was stopped by the police and in no uncertain terms expressed to them the rage she felt toward her husband. That was a mistake: while the Needham police are very far from quick-tempered, there are limits to the drunken abuse which they feel tolerable. After about twenty minutes of billingsgate from Jane, which severely complicated their efforts to persuade her to lock up her car and take a cab home, they took her in and locked her up.

Jane, to my resultant distress, made the call she was allowed, to Ellen, getting us both up at two o'clock in the morning, or thereabouts. Since Jane was still thoroughly drunk, we had considerable difficulty finding out where she was, although, to be sure, there was no trouble at all deducing what had brought her into that predicament. Instead of responding to my inquiries — Ellen was listening on the bedroom extension — Jane contented herself with reiterating: "Gotta have lawyer. You're gonna be my lawyer. Down and get me out. Gotta have a lawyer. You're gonna be my lawyer. Don't know any other lawyers." To this monologue Ellen contributed a counterpoint: "You've got to help her, Comp, you've got to go down there and help her."

I'm afraid I became thoroughly exasperated with both of them. Still on the phone with Jane, I said: "Ellen, don't be ridiculous. Go down there? She could be in Providence or Atlanta, for all I know. And anyway, I'm not going anywhere at this hour of night. We don't handle that kind of case, if it's what I think it is, and it is. We have a firm that we refer all such matters to, and if this woman can only gather her senses long enough to tell me where she is, I'll have him and a bondsman on their way in ten minutes."

Ellen was furious. Jane was her friend. Jane needed a lawyer. I was a lawyer. Jane asked her friend for help, and I'd embarrassed her by refusing to give it. For days I explained to her, over and over again, that I was brand-new to the firm, that the firm had a policy of long standing, never to undertake the representation of defendants in criminal cases, that we always referred them out to Walter Mahoney's office, and that while I might not approve of the rule, myself (I did, and I was very much opposed to its change, eight or nine years later; although I understood the necessity for the change, I resented it), I lacked the authority to change it and the foolhardiness to flout it. When, in 1968, the campus experiences of our hiring partner, Ed Foley, forced us to the consensus that we would be shut out of competition for the best graduating students unless we modified our policy and permitted them to engage in *pro bono publico* representation of indigent defendants in criminal cases, and conscientious objectors in military draft cases, I went along only after Larry Cable reminded me of my father's maxim: "A law firm is an organism, not a mechanism. The alternative to growth is atrophy."

If anything, though, I have occasionally wondered if we, through the years, have not reposed somewhat excessive faith in that proposition. From the two-man days of Carson Wills and Theodore Harper, to the 1920s when my father worked with between seven and ten other men under the firm name of Wills, Cable & Marshall, through the thirties, when about sixteen practiced in the office, and into the forties, when returning veterans combined with those who had remained in practice during the war to bring the firm to about thirty lawyers, and the change of its name to Wills, Cable, Cable & Chambers, the pace of growth was comparatively moderate. The degree of change was relatively manageable. And, perhaps most significantly, changes were instituted in response to the requirements of the practice, and not in submission to ideological or philosophical extortion.

I have said that my father did not compete with Carson Wills for the assignment to represent the firm's clients in court. That was, I am sure, somewhat of a sacrifice. Dad had the bearing, the temperament, the intelligence and the fortitude for the work, and his later career demonstrated those qualities. But it was the sort of sacrifice which the partners, in the early 1920s, believed themselves to have the right to require, for the good of the firm and thus for their mutual welfare. Wills, Cable, as we in the firm have always called it, whatever the mutations that have appeared upon the letterhead, was engaged in the general practice of law. But for that practice to be successful, the members of the firm had to parcel out the various areas of the law among themselves, and thus afford themselves the time to master each area, as specialists, to a point which the generalist could not hope to reach. Harry Cable, when he and Granddad started the firm, matured into one of the preeminent estate and trust specialists in the Commonwealth; for decades, his manual on estate planning was the standard work of reference for Massachusetts practitioners. Granddad concentrated on trial work, with similar results. One partner, in the first twenty years of this century, became the recognized authority on rights of way, thus justifying the substantial fees paid by the railway companies. Another branched out into personal injury work, and so on.

Each of those men was admitted to the firm because he was diligent, talented and resourceful. Not because he was black, Catholic, Jewish, handicapped, or because someone in Washington had decided that a company employing men must also, like it or not, employ women.

Nobody, in those years, went to work for Wills, Cable, under the erroneous impression that he had some sort of right to be there, nor that he would remain there if he saw fit to malinger, nor that the revenues of the firm were just as much his right as his reward, nor that he could dictate to the partners who had built the firm the conditions under which he would work or the tasks he would perform.

Cable Wills entered Wills, Cable, as the son of a founding

partner, yet he would never have dreamed of declaring that he insisted on being assigned cases to try, as perfectly unknown quantities do to Ed Foley each year when he interviews at the law schools for new associates. And that was not because my father lacked courage: it was because he lacked temerity, and was sensible enough to see that his own prosperity depended upon the prosperity of the firm, which required that he advance its ability to acquire new business by advancing its collective ability to discharge existing business successfully. Leaving the courts to my grandfather, whatever he might personally have preferred, he developed a new specialty, and all prospered in consequence.

That specialty was, incidentally, how my father became acquainted with Henry Morgan. He did not go out in search of Henry Morgan. He did not inquire into Henry Morgan's background, when Morgan sought to retain the firm, to satisfy himself that this gentleman desiring legal representation was fit also to serve as a vestryman, judge or molder of public opinion. Whatever Morgan may have been in those days, whatever he may be today, I can state categorically that my father never performed for him any services that were not strictly lawful, and comporting with the canons of legal ethics.

Indeed, I can go beyond that: I am sure that Morgan never asked him to do anything shady, because my father would at once have ordered him from the office, with a declaration that he would shortly receive a bill for all services and a written notice that the firm of Wills, Cable, would no longer represent him. And, furthermore, I am certain that if Morgan, then, was engaged in reprehensible conduct, my father was not aware of it: for years, with his full concurrence, Wills, Cable, referred out all divorce actions involving clients who had come to the firm before their domestic sadnesses occurred, and refused to undertake the representation of prospective clients who came in for the first time, seeking representation in divorces.

It was not because the members of the firm were unsympathetic to the situations of such people; it was because the members of the firm disapproved of divorce on moral and ethical grounds and believed themselves constrained to observe such standards in their professional as well as their private lives (that rule was abrogated in 1963, when Larry Cable, in a most perplexing and uncharacteristic act, determined, to the astonishment of both his father and my own, to obtain a divorce from his wife, Martha, and proffered in explanation this astonishing statement: he was doing it because he was damned sick and tired of her, and that was all there was to it. The firm did not handle his case, of course; Martha went to Reno, and he obtained his own representation. For a time there was some concern that he had taken leave of his senses. Harrison Cable and my father — Dad told me as a cautionary tale, when I reported my engagement to Ellen — were seriously apprehensive that it might be necessary to request Larry's resignation, but while he was somewhat cantankerous until the matter was concluded, there was no evidence that his intelligence or good judgment in representing clients was in any way impaired, and after reflection, it was decided that consistency required only that the rule against divorce work should be abandoned. That was when Mark Dunnigan was hired, and what he was brought in to do).

It was precisely that scrupulous balance of ethics, principles, practice and policy which I have never been able to convey intelligibly to Ellen, and that was why, as we entered the Hole with the Great Ledge to port, I was absolutely enraged at Andrew. Clearly recalling my arguments with Ellen about Jane, with the quarrels about Creighton still fresh in mind, I knew what was in store for me, now that he had mentioned

Henry Morgan. If she had been unable to accept Ted Fullerton as my client, because his research company was looking into something which might, just might, expedite a military victory for the United States, in some small way, then she would certainly have a great deal to say about the likes of Henry Morgan.

In that condition, mindful of Andrew's habit of baiting people, I was unprepared for his next sally, and had some enormous difficulty in controlling my temper.

If it had not been dark, I would have had some warning. Andrew, the vaudevillian, thinks it amusing to mock more than just the Southerners at the paper. He has another act, in which he clenches his teeth and talks through them, pronouncing words in what he evidently considers to be a sidesplitting exaggeration of the inflection and diction which my father, mother and, indeed, virtually everyone with whom I am friendly, uses. He pronounces *pretty* as *prit-tay*. He puts the stress on the first syllable of a word, and elides the second. It enrages me, and he knows it, which, of course, is why he does it. As we picked up the range of green lights that we would follow safely through the dark into the anchorage behind the drawbridge at Eel Pond, Andrew said, in that goddamned burlesque accent:

"I say, Daniel, d' you re*cawl* that *day*, when you put the *Tulip* aground heah? Your dad was frightfully pissed, as I remember. Insolent little *pup-pay* you were then, chap, eh? No charts and all."

I could have killed him. In as level a tone as I could manage, I said: "Goddamn you, Andrew. You never forget anything, do you? I was twenty years old when that happened. That was almost twenty years ago, and you still bring it up again. You never forget, do you? And you never let anyone else forget, either."

For a while he did not answer. I thought I had quelled him. But again, I was mistaken. In the darkness he said: "Two things there are, Daniel, that you above all people should know and remember: I always find out, and I never forget." At least he dropped the accent when he said it.

VIII

As I HAVE SAID, the three years or so that elapsed between my mother's death, and the night I met Ellen Shipp Hadley, were terrible torment for me. It was more than just grief, although that certainly was involved; I missed my mother terribly. I dreaded holidays and summers because it meant that I would be deprived of the companionship of my friends at school; for those who lived too far away to make the trips at Christmas and Easter, I felt almost envy, because when I went home, the house and her surroundings made me miss her all the more. But added to that, almost to the point at which I could not bear it, was the fact that I had no one else. Not that anyone else could have taken her place, because no one could, but I had no one else in whom to confide. I was suffering not only grief, but from loneliness. My father could be of scant assistance: he missed her too.

I dwell upon this (Ellen has said, perhaps somewhat morbidly) not only because it explains in some measure my gratitude for her, and reliance upon her (many times, when I have found myself involved with Mark Dunnigan in a conference about how a client's corporation, which I advise, will be affected by his divorce, which Dunnigan is handling, I have found myself speculating that the contending spouses simply never needed each other enough to appreciate each other fully. Mark does a lot of that work, now; it's numerically the largest part of the firm's business, though not, of course, monetarily; he always looks a little baffled), but also because it exposes the full subtlety of Andrew's cruelty. And, for that matter, his ingratitude.

When my father came into Wills, Cable, in 1920, still in law school but supplementing his instruction with the additional experience of being a clerk, he was assigned to the sundry matters of the Standard Oil Company of New York. There were a lot of them. As the automobile gained speedily in popularity, filling stations (as they were then called), and storage depots, had to be proliferated as well. There were maritime problems, resultant from the shipment of fuels, and as the shift from coal to oil heat began, additional problems of tank storage underground, by home heat dealers just starting in business.

Regulation then, thank God, was nowhere near as pervasive as it is today. Zoning boards in many towns did not exist. The choruses of complaint and dispute which now seem to form almost spontaneously, had never been inspired. If the police and fire departments were satisfied of the provisions for safety which the manufacturers and distributors had devised, the project was generally successful. The consumers, then, did not think of themselves as consumers. They wanted the product, and would pay reasonable prices to have it available where they needed it.

Nevertheless, there were problem areas, and here I must be very circumspect: I am relying on my father's memory, eked out with a bit of my own, of facts more than twenty years old when I heard them from him, and the only corroboration I can give is that I recall certain experiences which could indicate that he had at least the names of the participants aright. And, while the statute of limitations has certainly run on any improper business which others conducted, it will not do to impugn the departed.

When my father, then still in law school, had reviewed the Socony file, and familiarized himself with all of the problems then current, he made a list of them by category. By far the greatest number had their locus in the northeastern corner of one of the New England states. So many, in fact, that he was prompted to obtain a map, and to mark each place on it where one of this number of problems had arisen. Then, when he was finished, he drew a circle, using a compass, which included all of the dots he had placed on the map, and found that it was less than fifty miles across. His calculations showed that almost fifty percent of the company's most persistent problems in New England arose out of storage and distribution points proposed for that area. On a cost basis, about one-third of the money which Socony paid to Wills, Cable, each year, was for legal services performed with respect to locations within the circle.

His curiosity was aroused. Without speaking to anyone in the firm — for which omission, by the way, he told me he was severely rebuked, and deservedly so — he instituted certain inquiries. Their results intrigued him further: Socony's competitors were similarly situated in what he had come for convenience to call the "Horse-drawn Circle," but since he had been very discreet, none of them had yet perceived the oddity, even after he investigated.

Intentionally at first allowing Granddad Carson to believe that he was absent from the office because attending classes or doing research, later by outright deception, my father disguised from even the firm his extensive movements throughout the New England area. "I did some things that I shouldn't've done," he admitted to me. "I used an alias, but it was always the same alias. One day I said I was from the Maryland Asphalt Company, and I was looking around to see if my company should be submitting bids to pave roads in the area, and that seemed to go over all right, so I stuck to that, too. There was, you see, absolutely no question in my mind but that something was going on, and I had a pretty good idea what it was, too. But I didn't know who was doing it, and I thought it might be interesting if I found out. Still, I was not going to find out by walking in there and telling them I was a clerk and what was the fellow's name, please? No point in that. I had to make them come to me. So by using the same name, and the same explanation, everywhere I went, I made things a little easier for them, but not so easy that they might get suspicious.

"That went on," Dad said, "for about six months. I remember that I missed the Yale Game that year, because I was out looking at the foliage, and a good many other things as well. At the law school I said I was clerking; at the office I encouraged them to think I was at school. And I waited.

"In the spring of nineteen twenty-one," Dad said, "I know it was in April, but I do not know the day, I was actually in the office, plugging away at some problem or other, and your grandfather came into the library with a very funny look on his face. 'There's a man in my office,' he said. 'He's been here before. He won't give his name. He gave mine at the door, as, I am informed, he has done before, when I have been in court. He has done this three times in the past month. Today he was admitted, because I happened to be in. "You're not the fellow," he said.'

" 'What do you mean, sir,' I said. 'You asked for Mister Wills, and I am Mister Wills.'

" 'You may be Mister Wills,' he said, 'but you are not the fellow.'

" ' 'He seems to be a foreigner,' my father said," Dad told me. " 'British, I should think. I said to him: "I believe that you must have the wrong office."

" ' "Younger fellow," ' he said. ' "There another Mister Wills in here?" '

" 'Now, I ask you,' Granddad said, 'do you know this fellow?'

"I played dumb," Dad said. "I played dumb because I was scared. I said I didn't know if I knew him, because I hadn't seen him.

"Well," Dad said, "I knew him all right. I'd heard about him. Not what he looked like, not who he was, not where he came from and not how he talked, but I knew who he was. He was the man who had things to be taken care of, and until they were taken care of, the Horse-drawn Circle was going to remain.

"It was a fairly tense interview," Dad said. "At least at first it was. Your Granddad was very suspicious, and for that matter, so was I. My entire strategy had been bottomed upon the notion that there was something going on that was not quite right; its vindication, while marginally satisfying, did not reassure the participants, even though I had done it to smoke them out, and had succeeded.

"It was not that he was particularly menacing," Dad said. "He was rather fussily dressed, not much above average height, ruddy-complected, average weight for a man strongly built, a small, well-trimmed brown moustache. He held a bowler in his hand. He did have an accent, as your Granddad had said, but it was not readily identifiable. He had a very husky voice, which may have explained it.

" 'What is your business with my son?' your Granddad said. The man refused to say. 'It's a private matter.' He was very suspicious, and the visitor was equally taciturn. Your Granddad, with a client waiting, left us, albeit very reluctantly. We went into the library. He introduced himself. His name was Henry Morgan.

"I think that is about where I will leave it," Dad said, after a protracted pause. "We had some discussion, very circumlocutious on both sides, I can assure you. Then, without my vouchsafing any confidential business of my client, or his proposing anything improper, he left. Oh, yes, I was inexperienced enough, in those days, to inquire of people the causes of their peculiarities which interested me. It was several years before I bridled that inquisitiveness, and then only because I permitted myself that latitude in a matter before the Federal Communications Commission, and received a most unexpected reply. I met Mister Morgan before that experience.

" 'I am a citizen of the world,' he said. 'Where I adopted the accent, I cannot say. The tone of my voice is more certain. That I acquired in the Forest of the Argonne.' That, I discovered, was a lie. He had never served. 'I am a subject of the Crown.'

"At the time," Dad said, "I was as ready to believe that as I was anything else that he might have said: not very. But I was rash enough to do something, still without authority, on the basis of what he said, to arrange a confidential meeting of men several years my senior, who represented various parties, some in the legal capacity, others as officers, agents and employees. But all of them were connected with the oil business.

"We convened in a room at the Parker House, which I had reserved under the name of Michael Walker, of the Maryland Asphalt Company. I paid for it myself. When all had arrived, I introduced myself, giving my own name. I explained that Mr. Walker had been detained elsewhere, and had asked me to deliver his remarks.

"These were older men, and they all knew each other. They did not know me, although they knew your Granddad. They were not accustomed to lectures from those twenty or thirty years their junior, and they were consequently very puzzled.

"I must admit," Dad said, "that I took considerable personal pleasure from their confusion.

"I told them what they already knew. Remember this," my father told me, "and never forget it: the surest way to impress someone is to tell him the meaning of facts that he already knows. These were men successful at their business. Each of them had, at his fingertips, the facts appropriate and necessary to the management of his particular sphere. None of them, of course, would have disclosed any of them, in the company of men representing his competitors. Consequently, of all of the men in that room, only I had a sufficiently complete grasp of the details to extract from them their full significance. Each of them had individually assumed that the problems of his company, in the Horse-drawn Circle, were unique to his company; while each was very careful to commit no act detrimental to the industry as a whole, none trusted any of the others, and that, of course, accounted for the ability of their enemies to frustrate all of them.

"I will be more candid than perhaps I ought to be," my father said. "There is a widespread presumption that guile is only practiced in the city. It is incorrect. A small group of men in a strategic, though rustic, setting, had combined their political industry to penetrate a natural market, though not a large one, and to inconvenience, seriously, the industry's efforts to serve contingent marketing areas. They did not announce their intentions, and, publicly, there was no noticeable alliance among them. But the inescapable inference to be drawn from their behavior, ostensibly individual as it was, was that no oil company would find itself able to conduct its business in their areas until all of them were bribed.

"Today," my father said, "a combination such as that could not succeed, because the companies are nowhere near as dependent upon rail transportation, and highway transportation of their products is so much more rapid. But in those days, successful operation of the business required provision of small storage facilities near every population center. Without the facilities, the markets could be discerned, but not served.

"The conspirators," my father said, "had banded together to assure that none of them would accede to the installation of a storage facility in his bailiwick. Had any of them buckled, all would have failed, because any company able to obtain one facility permit would have developed the market, and, I might add, to its own considerable profit as well as to the discomfort of its competitors. But those men were crafty, and they held firm. What was denied in one community, was similarly denied in all the rest. It was, I thought, remarkable that there were any motor vehicles at all in that area, given the difficulties that those men erected before all efforts to furnish fuel for them. And there was absolutely no realistic possibility whatsoever for effecting the development of an adequate market for home-heating oil.

"Having explained that to the men who attended my little meeting, I reported that a man identifying himself as one Henry Morgan, for whom I could not vouch, had visited my office, and strongly intimated that the resolution of problems mutual to those present was most readily to be accomplished by a conference with one Stephen Michael Dunnigan, Esquire.

I said that I had never met Mr. Dunnigan, but that he was said to be engaged in the practice of law in Lawrence, Massachusetts. And I said I could not vouch for him, either. Then I left. I did not do anything. I did not tell them to do anything. To this day, I cannot really be sure that anything was done. I have my suspicions, of course, but that is all.

"Well," Dad said, "I caught enough hell for that, from your Granddad, and from Harrison Cable, and nearly everyone else in sight or within earshot, to make me think that I was damned to hell for the rest of my life, and certainly for anything that was likely to come after. They found my protestations of innocence unconvincing, to say the least. I was roundly assured that I would be disbarred before I was admitted, and promised that if by some cataclysmic oversight I was admitted, I would not be welcome to practice with Wills, Cable. My father had some remarks to make which flattered neither your grandmother nor the iceman. I was dismissed from my clerkship, with the advice that I might as well remain at the law school, to keep myself occupied and out of harm's way until the authorities caught up with me, and put me into the penitentiary.

"I slunk off," Dad said. "I resolved never to approach the verge again; I did not think that I had gone beyond it, although I did concede that men of more experience than I, were satisfied that I had.

"Then a strange development occurred," Dad said. "The following Easter, when I returned home despite the considerable strain that your Granddad and I had found in our relationship in the interim, I found him markedly conciliatory. He noted that I was about to graduate, and saying that all was forgiven, on the understanding that no recurrence would be tolerated, invited me to join the firm.

"I was lucky," he said. "Be guided by my narrow escape." This was as I prepared to join the firm. "Always get authority.

Things are different now. What could've happened to me, might happen to you, if you're careless. As I know you won't be." He paused, ruminatively. "You know," he said, in 1962, "it's just the damnedest thing. I never really did find out who the hell Henry Morgan was, where he came from, what he did. And — it must've been a couple or three years later — by accident, one day, I was looking for something else at the shop, blundered into a file that your Granddad was still working on, and from it discovered that eight of the nine men in the room at the Parker House that day had brought their business, personal and company, to the firm, by the end of nineteen twenty-three. Funny business, law."

The firm did prosper in those years. Those were the years in which Carson Wills purchased the house in Milton. And they were also the years in which, while Granddad remained in the full vigor of his years, my father commenced to rival him as a business-getter for the firm. By the end of the decade, the Crash and all, my father was challenging Harrison Cable.

There is, really, no discernible pattern in the clients credited to my father during those seven years. There were two or three small banks, outside the city, which required minimal representation, having local counsel who apparently transacted the lucrative business of searching titles and passing papers on mortgaged land transactions.

The Franklin Automobile Company retained the firm, paid five hundred dollars, evidently required no counsel in Massachusetts that year, or got it elsewhere, and did not renew the agreement.

The Atlas Powder Company, of Wilmington, Delaware, checked in, in 1927, with what was then the hefty retainer of three thousand dollars, required — so far as I have been able to determine — no substantial expenditures of time, and renewed the following year, and every year thereafter. Atlas now retains us for an annual fee of ten thousand dollars a year, most of our time being devoted to the tedious business of knocking down the specious claims of cheap lawyers retained by cranks who believe that all their petty miseries were brought about the day the construction company ignited a perfectly placed and expertly detonated charge in some road-building project within a hundred miles of them.

During the thirties, also, we commenced representation of Westinghouse Electric, and the Aluminum Corporation of America.

Out of all that prosperity there came increased responsibilities for my father, many of them, apparently, requiring him to travel extensively. He was still a bachelor, then, living at the club and filling his days and nights with work which he enjoyed.

Early in the decade, from what I have been able to piece together, he became influential at a secondary level with the FCC, probably as a result of his work with Westinghouse, which was then moving into broadcasting. He appears to have spent a considerable amount of his time in Washington, and to have participated in certain aspects of the drafting of the Federal Communications Act of 1934.

Briefly, he handled a modest amount of business for various subsidiaries of the American Telephone & Telegraph Co., but there was some friction between Harrison Cable and one of its executives, and they sought new counsel. Harrison Cable had a temper, as my father used to say and had good reason to know.

But there was no cause for anyone to take alarm: my father's work for Socony had carried him into the higher reaches of Standard Oil, where his efforts met with the same national approval that had attended his regional work for the subsidiary, and by the end of 1934, he had commenced what was then a man-killing schedule of trips, here and abroad, for the parent company.

My efforts to determine the specific purposes of those journeys have been mostly unavailing. But there was a pattern, of sorts: after a period in Boston, he would travel to New York and lay over for two or three days, which suggests that he was attending conferences there. Then he would board a Cunarder for London. His letters and cables, now yellowed in the files, are cryptic, and show only that he lodged at Claridge's. On his return to New York, generally after a fortnight or so, he appears usually to have gone to Washington, staying a day or so, then returning to New York for what I assume to have been further conferences before returning to Boston. A fortnight or so later, he would be off again. The files are thin, but the billings were substantial. Whatever he was doing, Standard Oil was clearly pleased with it.

That pattern did not change after he married. Nor was there any reduction in his travel after I was born. It continued through the end of 1941, where there was a hiatus of about three months in his international travel — though the trips between Washington and Boston continued sporadically — and then resumed in the fall of 1942, this time with more protracted visits to London, hazardous though they had become. Petering out after the war was over, they were replaced with more extended stays in Washington. Dad was always diligent to be home for holidays, when I was young, but I reached the age of eight without much knowledge of him. I was not badly off: there were other boys who never saw their fathers, as the result of that conflict.

Nevertheless, I felt badly off, if I felt it at all. In retrospect I see (Ellen had taken enough courses to qualify for her Master's in psychology, although she has not completed her thesis, and I am afraid I have imbibed some of her jargon) that I struggled mightily to compensate for that, as I grew older. Indeed, the most vivid childhood recollection that I have of him, excepting the parties and the celebrations, is of the time when I was still quite young, and Benson drove us to Albany, Mother and me. We stayed at the DeWitt Clinton that night. The next day we boarded the *Hendrick Hudson* of the Hudson River Day Line, and sailed down to the pier around 120th Street in Manhattan, where he met us, and I was so very glad to see him. I ran to him, and he caught me and lifted me up. He came back to Albany with us, and we had duck in the dining salon, and then we rode back to Boston the next day, to Milton where Betsey and Andrew were almost as glad to see him as I had been. Everyone wanted to please him.

For the next twenty years and more — that was around 1949 or so — that purpose, I'm afraid, dominated my mind. And, oddly enough, I think it dominated his, also, passively instead of actively.

Until 1944, when Granddad died, leaving Dad the house in Milton, Mother and I had lived in the house he bought when they were married, in Brookline. It was a gray affair — I remember it only dimly — and there was a maroon sofa in the sitting room, upon which I was not allowed to sit. I had a dog, a Boston terrier, and Mother had Mrs. Mulready, who came in every morning, and stayed until dinner was prepared. We did not have a car, not, I guess, that it would have mattered much, considering rationing, but Granddad had Benson come out every Sunday to collect us for the trip to Milton, for dinner. Granddad had a Studebaker President, a 1939 model. When he died, we moved to Milton, and life continued in the main house.

We acquired the house at Duxbury in 1945, on the fourth of April, but my father was not there much, either, for the next six or seven years.

I think, now, that it was inadvertence. He simply did not perceive, in all those years, that he was away far more than he was present, and that Mother's valiance in refusing to protest, assisted him the more in his negligence.

Whatever the reason, it was as though her death had brought him, startled, to his senses. Betsey and Andrew, to be sure, were around, as company for me. But gradually, I used to think, he came around to the recognition that there was comparatively little between us, him and me, and began to make reparations.

The first of them was *Hyacinth*, a wooden seventeen-footer of local construction that drew about two and one-half feet and heeled like a cork. As though reclaiming his grandfather's heritage, my father sailed it expertly on Duxbury Harbor, and did his best to instruct me in the mystery.

He did not succeed, although for six or seven years we both pretended that he had. I insisted that I enjoyed the experience, when I hated it; there is apparently some oddity in my middle ear, which exaggerates the normal sensation of being off-balance, and absolutely terrifies me when I am in airplanes, or anything else not proceeding upon solid ground.

For his part, Dad pretended he was satisfied with the way I handled *Hyacinth*, and took vocal satisfaction in the genetic advantage which enabled me to adopt the sport so quickly and so well. I went along with him. He sold *Hyacinth*, when we moved to Nantucket, and ordered *Tulip*, to be delivered there.

We had a house in Monomoy, on the island (most do not know that there is a Monomoy on Nantucket in addition to the one on the Cape), the down payment made with the proceeds of the sale of the house in Duxbury. He said he intended the change to insure that isolation would guarantee long uninterrupted summers. But I was in law school, then, and he was otherwise alone except for Andrew and Betsey, far too intelligent a man to have so failed to take account of the events likely to occur as children grow older, and prepare to leave home. He purchased *Tulip*, a sloop of the Ensign class, faster and with a deeper draft, than *Hyacinth*.

It was, as Andrew said, the *Tulip* which I grounded, with my father and Ellen aboard, that summer so many years ago. I expected fury from my father. What he said was this: "I should've known better. It's Andy who's the sailor." Perhaps he thought I had been punished enough: to ground in Woods Hole is to hammer the hull on the table rocks. The *Tulip*, though towed in, awash, was damaged too badly to warrant repair. The three of us were lucky to have survived.

It was not my fault. The outboard quit as we bucked the current, and we were swept onto the rocks. "Most people," Dad said, "don't buck the current."

IX

It was nearly eight-thirty when we entered the channel that leads into Eel Pond. We had made a tight circle to port off the Oceanographic Institute, Andrew heading her up in the diminishing wind, watchful among the markers as Ellen furled the genoa and Deirdre and I dropped the main, wrapping it inside itself and securing it with the shock cords, Andrew keeping the engine at one-third speed. Behind us, as we worked, the *Islander* of the Steamship Authority docked a little after eight-fifteen, and the *Uncatena* appeared off Nobska Point, her lights bright in the evening trip from Oak Bluffs. Using the boat hooks, Deirdre on the port and I on the starboard kept the boat from the stone walls that confine the channel. Ellen gave two long and two short blasts on the horn.

"Provided he didn't decide to go home a little early," Andrew said.

The drawbridge began to rise, and the light to our left changed from red to green. We went through, carefully and at low speed, into the salt pond, Andrew shouting up to the man who tended the bridge: "*African Violet.* Collier. Nantucket. Thank you."

By then it was his, a fact which I understood as little, then, as I had understood my father's purchase of it, in the late persisting winter of 1970. Ex *Ariel*, it was a Hinckley Bermuda 40, launched originally in 1964 at Southwest Harbor, Maine, rigged as a yawl for a doctor from Stonington, Connecticut, named Jonathan Maxwell. Its hull was black, and its lines were and are beautiful, though its accommodations were cramped by the standards of the high-windage Morgans, Irwins and Gulfstars of the same approximate length. Doctor Maxwell, suffering what he clearly must have felt to have been a most premature heart attack, at age forty-three, had put it on the market in the fall of 1969, and retired to a Grand Banks 35 trawler yacht. With some relish, my father told me that the good doctor, consummating the sale at Burr Brothers Boat Yard, in Marion, Massachusetts, was scarcely able to conceal his fury at selling the boat to a man nearly thirty years older. It cost Dad sixty-three thousand dollars, in mint condition, worth every penny and probably more. He was very smug when he bought it, and I was utterly baffled.

Andrew in the darkness brought the boat smoothly through the pond, Deirdre on the foredeck with the hand lantern. When she spotted the mooring, she called out, and Ellen went forward to handle the light while Deirdre used the hook.

"We're on," she said, cleating the line down, and Andrew,

the engine in neutral, shut the power down. With the spreader lights of the mainmast on, I took down the mizzen sail, and we rode to the current, silent in the darkness. Andrew was allowed another drink.

"The Rachel Fletcher Paint Company," Andrew said, extending his legs in the cockpit and sliding far down on his tailbone, "was originally incorporated in nineteen thirty-one, with home offices in Wheeling, West Virginia, for the principal purpose of making, of all things, paint. Rachel Fletcher was the name of the wife of the guy that had the capital, and the other two guys were the people that thought up the process.

"Now here were three fairly unrealistic fellows," Andrew said, "starting a business in nineteen thirty-one, with Herbert Hoover's hand upon the tiller, and the economy so fundamentally sound there were a hell of a lot of people scrounging around in garbage cans, trying to get something to eat. But they made it, just the same, and the reason they made it was pure blind luck: they could make a good product a hell of a lot cheaper than anybody else could, and it lasted longer. In the pits of the Depression, if you could make a good paint, cheap, and sell it, cheap, you could find a lot of buyers who were painting things they never would've painted in good times, because they would've been tearing them down. Somehow, they were using coal to make paint, or coal wastes, or something that came out of the process that you use to make coke from coal: it was a secret process, not even patented, and it's been superseded now. But for about twenty years, it was the best thing around. Until they started making the latex stuff.

"Mister Rachel Fletcher and his buddies," Andrew said, "were very modest people, also. They didn't want the goddamned moon with a ring around it. What they wanted was enough money to give Mister Rachel a decent return on his investment, and the guys who thought the thing up a small windfall for their brilliance. Which, of course, they got, being shrewd enough to see that there was a period of limited duration for the uniqueness of their product. But not shrewd enough to see that because there was a war coming, a company that dealt in chemicals might be worth even more than a company that made paint, even if the company that was dealing in chemicals happened to be a company that made paint. Quotas and all.

"Some way or another," Andrew said, "Fletcher and his Frankensteins'd found a way to make paint, using butadiene. Don't ask me what the hell butadiene is, because I don't know, and I dunno what the hell they used it for. But they used it, and they had experience using it, and it was pretty likely, if you owned Rachel Fletcher Paint Company around the end of the thirties, and there was some reason why butadiene was gonna be rationed, you could get a ration of it.

"Now there're other things that you can use butadiene for," Andrew said. "You can spread it on your breakfast rolls, and you can use it for suntan lotion, or maybe it's some other things, but whatever they are, they include the manufacture of synthetic rubber. Fletcher and his dummies, if they knew that, didn't care. Sold out the company, secret processes, coal mines and all, for something in the neighborhood of a million bucks, to Royal Caribbean Industries, Limited, and went home, smug.

"You might well wonder," Andrew said in the darkness, "what the hell a Bahamian corporation would want with a West Virginia paint company. As, in fact, did I, thirty-seven years after the fact. But of course I knew something about Henry Morgan, in nineteen seventy-five; in nineteen thirty-eight, they obviously did not. Them being all dead, and their heirs as content with the deal as the people who made it had been, and fully ignorant of why Royal Caribbean wanted the little jerkwater thing in the first place, I assumed, as I always do, that it was probably the Mafia.

"And of course, I was right, for the same cockeyed reasons that I've been right before, and wrong before: because if you take any complicated deal, and you've got one-third of a suspicious mind, you can find the Mafia working behind the scenes as indeed they always are, but not necessarily as *mafiosi*.

"Now when I think I've got a line on the wise guys," Andrew said, "by a series of complicated maneuvers with which I will not bore you, I get in touch with my friend who likes to slip in and out of the McAlpin, and I did that. I met him there and he spared me eight minutes on a warm afternoon. I was careful to explain that the Bank of Sark story was on the back burner — when he gives you something, he does not like to see it neglected. Then I described to him what my preliminary investigations into the Rachel Fletcher Paint Company had turned up.

"Strangest reaction I ever got from the guy," Andrew said. "Rachel Fletcher didn't mean a fucking thing to him. I tried to jog him along. Nothing. And the guy does not lie to me. 'Look,' I said, 'I understand this is a Delaware corporation, now, with a Bahamian parent company, and Henry Morgan's involved.'

"All the blood went out of his face," Andrew said. "I mean it. This guy wouldn't blow his cookies if you threw the Strategic Air Command at him, but I thought I was gonna regret not bringing any digitalis. He stood up. 'You will be contacted,' he said, and he left.

"Three days later," Andrew said, "I was running up the phone bill at the office — this was about three weeks ago — trying to get somebody in the utilities field who could give me hard numbers about the actual mortality risks of nuclear power stations, and how close they come to the figures we've already got for fatalities on the highway that we seem to get

along with all right, and I get a call. Major General Aubrey
Gammage, United States Army, retired. 'Now what in the
name of God does this guy want?' I think. 'Hardening of the
arteries, probably.' I thought the voice sounded vaguely familiar, but from where I could not imagine. It was the guy
with the bad leg — the lame man. Passing through town, he
was staying at the Mayflower Hotel, despite the clatter of the
Metro construction on Connecticut Avenue.

" 'General,' I said, 'that's very nice. But what the hell do I
care?'

" 'I was passing through town,' he said, 'and I had heard of
your inquiries about Rachel Fletcher.'

"I was there in twenty minutes," Andrew said, "still laboring
under the impression that I was working on a story about coal,
and the people who dig it, and who owns it and them.

"He's really old, now, Dan," Andrew said. "He doesn't get
up when you enter the room, and when he has to get up, to go
to the bathroom, or something, he has to use two canes, and
it's only pride that makes him do that: he should have crutches.
His voice is gone. The only way that you can hear him on the
phone is because he's got his amplifier that he carries with him,
and hitches on the mouthpiece. When you talk to him in person, you're hunching forward in the chair all the time, and you
hate to ask him to repeat anything, because it's obviously so
hard for him to say it in the first place. He peers at you: I think
he's had cataracts, but I was afraid to ask because I thought it
might've been glaucoma, and he was going blind and there
was nothing he could do about it. Besides, he's still a tough old
motherfucker. You don't want to offend a guy like that.

" 'I don't have a breath to spare,' he said. 'I understand that
you've been prowling and snooping around.' Not your basic
tactful opening to a member of the working press, but at least

having the merit of reflecting accurately the mood of the speaker.

" 'That's one way of putting it,' I said.

" 'There's a good deal that you do not understand,' he said.

" 'General,' I said, 'there's a whole universe out there that I don't understand.' "

Andrew is always the self-deprecating hero of his own stories.

" 'I'm working at it, one aspect at a time. If I live long enough, I'll get, maybe, three or four of them. That'll leave the other millions. There's seven million stories in the naked city.'

" 'You are under the impression, I take it,' he said, 'that the Rachel Fletcher Paint Company is somehow connected with an international criminal cartel.'

"As a matter of fact," Andrew said, "I never dreamed of such a thing, if an international criminal cartel was different from the Cosa Nostra. If it was the same, I was *convinced* of it, but I wasn't used to being summoned by retired major generals to talk about the Cosa Nostra, and when I was, stunned as I was, I began at once to wonder if maybe it wasn't the Mafia at all, but an international criminal cartel that I'd never even heard of. Quick-witted as always, and dealing only with a man with sixty more years to carry than I had, I said: 'Not *somehow connected*. Connected through Henry Morgan.'

"That flushed him out," Andrew said. "I would imagine that General Aubrey Gammage was an extremely formidable fellow when he was younger, and he got the wind up him. Now he's limited by his years and his ailments, but he's still pretty impressive. He was furious. He sat there, croaking at me, and I thought he'd die before he finished. As a matter of fact, he was so goddamned unpleasant that I *hoped* he'd die before he finished. The old walrus.

" 'You understand nothing,' he said.

" 'It's hard to understand anything, when you don't know where the people are, who can give you the facts, and they persist in hiding out,' I said.

" 'No one is hiding out,' he said. He rasped.

" 'Look, General,' I said, 'no offense to years and experience, but I laid around and stayed around this old town too long. Summer's coming on. I can't find a guy, it's because the guy doesn't wanna be found. He doesn't wanna be found, I gather he doesn't wanna talk. There's an old rule in my line of work: there comes a time, you gotta go with what you got. I got this widely known buccaneer, that for some reason, I can't seem to locate. I think I'm gettin' close to that time.'

" 'Young man,' he said, 'you understand nothing.'

" 'I'se sittin' right here, Massa,' I said. ' 'Splain me. I listened to Ron Ziegler, I listened to a whole mess of white folks. You jes' ask around. I'll b'leeve anything. You just go right ahead and say what you got on your mind. I guarantee you, I'll believe it. I always do. Sometimes I even print it. But mostly, I look into it, first, 'count of how I'm so credulous and all, and I'm always gettin' taken in.'

"Have you," Andrew said, " — you're an experienced man, Daniel, well versed in many things, jack of all trades, master of many. Have you ever heard of *Buna-S?*"

I was still angry. I said: "No."

"Do you know what it is?" Andrew said.

I said: "No."

"Well," Andrew said. "I didn't, either. And I'm still not sure that I do. Well, I know what it is, I guess, but what the hell it's got to do with Rachel Fletcher, I do not know."

"Is that important?" I said.

"Yes," he said. "*Buna-S* is a kind of rubber. Not the kind that protected you from infection while you were at Exeter, and me from enforced interruption of my studies at Milton High, like

Trojans and all the rest of them nasty things. As a matter of fact, *Buna-S* isn't really, wasn't really, even rubber at all. But if you mixed it with things, like oil and coal and alcohol and shit like that, you would get rubber. Synthetic rubber. How's that hit ya, Daniel?"

In the darkness I remained perplexed, and said so.

"Well," Andrew said triumphantly, "for once we got common ground. That's pree-zactly what I done said to the General. I said: 'What the fuck is *Buna-S?*' And you know what that man said to me? He said: 'I'll answer that, young fellow, but on one condition.'

" 'And what's that, General, sir?' I said.

" 'You agree to get the whole story, before you print anything,' he said. 'All of it. Whatever it takes. And to let me review what you've written, before it appears.'

"Until he got to the second part," Andrew said, "I thought I had died and went to heaven. I finally had Priddy, right where the hair's short and curly, if it was worth doing. 'Review it?' I said.

" 'Not censor it,' the General said. 'Just review it. So we'll, so I'll know what it's going to be. Everyone concerned is quite old now, and most of our adversaries are dead, or so well advanced in years as to be as ineffectual as I am, now, or I would thrash you within an inch of your life for your impertinence. But if you misrepresent us, decrepit as we are — and we are willing to take that chance — surely we must be conceded the opportunity to be prepared to rebut what you have to say. Not to say it before you have spoken, but to be prepared to respond to it after it is said.'

" 'Not censorship,' I said.

" 'Nor prior restraint,' he said. 'Equal time. We're old enough, now, to take our chances, and if we lose, well, we won enough.'

"You never do what I did," Andrew said. "Oh, I asked for something more, and I got it. But you never even suggest you're hooked, and I was and I did. 'What do I get for this?'

" 'Why,' the old bastard said, 'your story. Whatever you want to write. Of course, if it's wrong, we'll destroy you.'

" 'Who the hell am I dealing with?' I said.

"He did the best he could to laugh at me, choking and coughing, carrying on at a great rate. Finally he stopped. 'It's not like the old days, young man,' he said. 'Not like the old days at all, I'm sorry to say. We will simply do everything in our power to see to it that your career is ruined.' He leaned forward, and hissed it out like a big puff adder: '*Destroyed.*'

"I wasn't taking that," Andrew said. "I got up. 'Forget it,' I said, 'this kind of shit I can nicely do without. See ya around, Gramps.'

"He began to laugh. It was the goddamnedest laugh you ever heard. 'Fine,' he said, 'fine,' and I was halfway to the door before it occurred to me: I was probably doing exactly what he wanted."

The stars were scattered in the sky, and the sky was velvet blue, and the lights of Woods Hole were beginning to soften in a night mist. I waited impatiently for Andrew to come to the point; there was beef Stroganoff in the icebox below, and some red wine and French bread and sweet butter. We had been all day long at sea, which I hated, and I had subsisted on breakfast ashore and a rather scanty ham sandwich at lunch. I felt I had humored, suffered, and endured Andrew long enough for one day. I had had enough, for a man not even sure why he'd been summoned.

" 'Aw right,' I said, and I turned around," Andrew said, " 'what the hell am I dealing with?'

" 'The Rachel Fletcher Paint Company,' he said, wheezing all over the place.

" 'La Cosa Nostra,' I said.

"I thought he was gonna have a spasm," Andrew said. " 'Perhaps,' he said. 'The tanks in Sicily, after all, came off the LSTs with red flags flying from their antennas.' "

"I don't get it," Ellen said.

"Lucaina," Andrew said. "Salvatore Lucaina, Lucky Luciano's flag. He was deported, by his own request, after he handled the New York dock strike. Means nothing. Maybe: means nothing. 'Well,' I said, 'am I?'

" 'Young man,' he said, oh he was having a wonderful time for himself, or else he was conning me left and right, and I was going for it, 'young man, believe what you wish. You will do so, anyway.'

"I did it," Andrew said. "I'm a walkin', talkin' doll, and I crawls on my belly like a snake. I stopped. He had me. 'I gotta have more,' I said. 'I can't get the go-ahead on what I got now, and you're old enough to know, I got to have a green light.'

"He nodded," Andrew said. "If I ever saw a nod of satisfaction, of resignation and delight in the human condition, that was it. He nodded again. 'I got to know who I'm dealing with,' I said, 'and what I'm dealing for, and who's in the wings, and I have to be able to tell people, at least that much.'

"For a while he didn't say anything," Andrew said. "Then he began to wheeze and cough and complain without saying anything, hacking and spuming away. Then he said: 'I like a man who knows his own mind.' Sarcastic bastard. 'I'll give you two things, and one name, and an invitation. You have one month to investigate the two things. The name, you already know: *Predecessor; Dreamland.*'

" 'What's the name?' I said. I was sure he was nuts, by then.

" 'I told you,' he said, cackling and wheezing after he did it. 'You know the name. You always have.'

" 'Is it Morgan?' I said.

" 'Morgan is the name you will reach, if you obtain authority to proceed,' he said. 'I will relent. I will provide a third thing, for your investigation: *Gentian.*' Then he laughed again, and Jesus, Deirdre, it was awful when he laughed. 'As a matter of fact, young man, you already know most of it. But you don't know you know it. I will call you in a month.'

"I was dismissed," Andrew said, "and I left. I stopped at the Class Reunion, where all us tough correspondents hang out, and I had nineteen beers and kept my mouth shut. Did I have a daffy old man? Or did I have something? A daffy old man, was my conclusion. I went home.

"The next morning," Andrew said, "I woke up with a headache, and a vast impatience with garrulous old men, and made the mistake of calling Deirdre, here, and . . . tell them what you said to me, Deirdre."

"Not much of anything, really," Deirdre said.

"Except," Andrew said, " '*Gentian.* Is that code?' I called my friend in New York again, from a pay phone to a drop, to a pay phone from the pay phone, of course. Simple prudence. Because that's the only way he'll talk to me, or anybody else, as far as that's concerned. Genuinely baffled. 'Never heard of no *Predecessor*,' he said. 'That a horse or something?' And how about *Gentian?* 'Same thing.' *Dreamland?* 'That a place on Third Avenue or something, singles' bar?' Shit.

"Then," Andrew said, "I had a brainstorm, and it was even really that. 'All right,' I said, '*Buna-S*' What the hell is *Buna-S?*' He had no more trouble with that'n he would've had with giving me the spread on the Mets and the Giants, Seaver pitching. 'Synthetic rubber,' he said. 'It's a thing they use in synthetic rubber. Used to use in it. Know who could tell you about *Buna-S?* Henry Morgan. You can find Henry Morgan, you got *Buna-S.*'

"Well," Andrew said that night in the peaceful harbor, "naught happens unless soul clap hands and sing. I started out with a shit story about coal, and I did it, and I got a lead on Henry Morgan, and I did the coal story and there I was, back to Henry Morgan. 'All right,' I said, ever the cooperative sort, 'where the fuck do I find the pirate Morgan?'

" 'Shit,' he said, 'I dunno. The last I heard of him, he was fucking around with something quiet in the Caribbean.'

" 'And what might that've been?' I said.

" 'I dunno,' he said. I could tell he was lying, even by phone. 'Look, you ask me something, I always tell you what I know. I tell you I dunno, means: I dunno. I dunno, is all.'

" 'Heard anything more about bonds?' I said," Andrew said. "It was like I made *him* think, for a minute. If he was faking me, he was doing it superbly well. 'No,' he said, 'no, as a matter of fuckin' fact, I haven't. I wonder why the hell that is?'

" 'You wanna go and find out?' I said. 'Call me back?' There was a long silence. 'No, as a matter of fact,' he said, 'I don't think I do.'

"Well," Andrew said, "needless to say, I did. By now I was being so rude to Priddy, I don't think I would have stood for what I did, myself. I was never there. I was all over the place. I don't know why it didn't occur to me sooner: I guess I just thought that anything that Henry Morgan was tied up with must be so exotic that nobody else in the world'd ever know what the fuck it was. Until one day a week and a half ago, when I was out at the Food and Drug Administration, and they had this release on how they're okaying Phenylbutazolidine, for prescription to people that've got gout.

"The press officer's a nice broad," Andrew said. "I was horsing around with her, so to speak, and I said to her: 'Same stuff Dancer's Image had for the Derby?' 'Pretty much,' she said.

'Son of a bitch,' I said, if I take this stuff, instead of jogging a mile in the morning, I'll take a mile and six furlongs, and do it in one-forty-eight, flat.' 'Easy,' she says, and we were still hacking around. . . ."

"You were trying to pick her up," Deirdre said.

"I was trying to pick her up," Andrew said, "you being out of town and all, and it just came into my head: 'This anything like *Buna-S*?' 'Hell, no,' she said. '*Buna-S* is a butadiene process. Hasn't been of much importance since World War Two.' And why was it important then? 'Shit,' she says. . . ."

"Foul-mouthed broad," Deirdre said.

". . . the foul-mouthed broad," Andrew said, " 'I'm no fuckin' chemist' — she didn't actually use that adjective, but I hate to disappoint the audience — 'you know. It was for tires.' The hell're tires so important? 'Look,' she said patiently, 'I'm no fuckin' chemist, but you're no fuckin' historian.' She didn't say that, either, not in those words. But she was right. 'You got any idea, what happened, World War Two?'

" 'Not a hell of a lot,' I said, in my winning way.

" 'Well,' she said, 'have I got news for you. The Japs invaded Malaya, and a lot of other places.'

" 'After Pearl Harbor,' I said.

" 'After Pearl Harbor,' she said. 'But *before* Pearl Harbor, people were worrying about them invading Malaya, and shutting off Singapore, and all them other good things."

" 'So what?' I said.

" 'So,' she said, 'when they did it, they shut off the latex, and all of a sudden we hadda build a mechanized army, from scratch.'

" 'We did it,' I said. "I always heard that, anyway,'

" 'And what'd it roll on?' she said. 'Wheels, maybe?'

" 'Tires,' I said.

" 'Tires,' she said. 'Synthetic rubber. *Buna-S*. Go look it up.'

" 'Why the hell should I look it up?' I said.

" 'Because,' she said, '*Buna-S* was a German patent.'

" 'So what?' I said.

" 'Standard Oil was the American licensee,' she said. 'The outfit that owned the process wouldn't let Standard use it here, and I think they stalled it off for about three or four years. Get ahold of some lawyer; they all know about it. I think the thing was tied up in court for a couple years.'

"I did that," Andrew said. "I went to see a gentleman of the bar who can tell you anything you need to know about anything that's happened in Our Nation's Capital, as we so fondly call it, since Tommy the Cork got himself an office and a desk and went to work for FDR. On one condition: you can only use what he tells you to sharpen your questions for somebody else, who can be quoted directly but never would be, of course, otherwise, because you wouldn't be shrewd enough to make up the questions and trap him if you didn't talk to my guy first.

" 'Why, yes,' he said, leaning back in his chair. Wonderful man, very handsome and big, slow-moving, slow-talking, beautiful disguises for very high-speed thinking, 'that was I. G. Farben. When Standard requested authority to duplicate the *Buna-S* process here, Farben declined.' He wraps his tongue and lips around delicious ironies. ' "For reasons of military expediency." And that was in *nineteen thirty-nine*. The Wehrmacht was adequately supplied with synthetics, so that it did not matter to the Jerries if they should by some mischance be denied access to natural rubber, whether by Japanese whim or naval interdiction. We were not. Now it would seem to me,' he said, 'that the Farben response should have occasioned immediate apprehension, inasmuch as there were existing at that time no military exigencies *between* us, at least, and for the further reason that Farben evidently had information to the effect that there would soon be, at very least, military exigencies against somebody else. Lend–Lease, if that were the reason, could mean by its tacit citation only that Britain and France were threatened, because the Germans had the nonaggression pact with Stalin.

" 'Do you know what was done about that?' he said. 'For more than two years, nothing was done, because Standard in great piety declined to use the process without Farben's permission. *After* Pearl Harbor. After the Battle of Britain had begun. Indeed, four months after we had gone to war against Germany, herself. Why, Thurman Arnold had to bring an antitrust action to part Standard from its monopoly of *Buna-S* patents. And do you know what reason Standard gave for this? "International legal and business ethics." '

"He shook his head," Andrew said. " 'Most of the legal problems of large businesses have very little to do with the law, whether in origin or in solution, and the same might be said of their problems with public contempt.'

"That still didn't lead me to Henry Morgan," Andrew said. "Therefore, I asked him: 'And where does a man named Henry Morgan fit into all of this?'

"He was uncertain at first. Tilted back in his chair, clasped his hands behind his head, thought about it. 'Henry Morgan,' he said. 'Henry Morgan.'

" 'Used to work out of Nassau,' I said.

" 'Oh,' he said, 'I know who he is. I'm quite familiar with him, actually. Morgan's a British subject who's found our laws of incorporation, and those of the Bahamas, far better suited to his purposes than those of England herself. Or the way in which they are administered, at least. A small, dapper and dishonest man, seldom in the thick of things, for years and years he stalked the fringes of the larger killings, making off with scraps. Although, of course, those were very considerable scraps. But what he might have had to do with *Buna-S*, I cannot quite frankly imagine.'

"I was disappointed, and it showed. I tried out Rachel Fletcher on him, and it meant nothing to him. He shook his head, very slowly. 'No, no,' he said, 'I never heard of it. You know, it's a pity Cable Wills is dead. Indeed, I understood that he elected to remain as counsel for Morgan when confronted with the choice of severing that relationship, or losing a very substantial account, during the war.'

" 'What account?' I said. 'Well,' he said, 'really, this is only gossip, together with surmise, but I must confess I was intrigued enough when I heard it to inquire, very delicately, of course, of Cable, if Standard had selected a different law firm for New England. And — he was a marvelous man, Cable, a fighter. When he was with the OWI, the Office of War Information, our clients in publishing and broadcasting invariably received quick, clear, correct answers to their questions. Quite frequently they did not like those answers, and dispatched me to endeavor to change Cable's mind.' He sighed. 'It was seldom possible. He had a sure instinct for his ground, and it is hard to argue with a man who thinks he's right, and does not fear your retribution. Cable said that Standard had indeed determined to change counsel, and jutted out his jaw, in that way he had.

" 'Well, sir,' he said, 'when Cable was ready for a fight, it would have contravened God's will to deny him his pleasure. So I pressed on: And had Standard, as I had heard, left Wills, Cable, because he had refused to dissociate himself from Henry Morgan?

" 'He was genuinely, I am sure, genuinely astonished. I often saw Cable Wills angry, but never deceitful. "Good heavens, no," he said. "Good Heavens, I wish it had been something so trivial as that. No, this was a substantial and irreconcilable difference over policy matters." Then my dear wife, we were conversing at a dinner party at Senator Wheeler's — this was around the middle of nineteen forty-two — beckoned to me, and I of course responded, and Cable and I never did finish our conversation. Cable would be able to tell you a good deal about Henry Morgan.'

"I was pretty frustrated by then," Andrew said. " 'Good God,' I said, 'I'm at the point now where I'd settle for somebody who could just tell me where the guy is.'

" 'Where he is?' he said. 'Well, that should be easy enough.' He punched the intercom button. This woman who looked like all librarians should look, very prim, about sixty-five, at least. 'Miss Springer,' he said, after forty years they still don't use first names to each other, 'would you see if you can locate our current address for Henry Morgan.'

"She faltered," Andrew said. " 'Yes, sir,' she said. 'Forgive me, sir, but the cards are filed separately. Is his under *Predecessor?*'

" 'No,' he said, 'no, *Predecessor* is closed. It's under *Gentian.*'

"I almost shit," Andrew said. " '*Gentian?*' I said. He smiled. 'We're rather set in our ways now, I'm afraid. Habits of long standing are cherished in and of themselves, as though by the very fact of their longevity they furnished contradictions of the very premise they imply: intimations of mortality. You understand that while I do not especially admire Henry Morgan, more than thirty years' experience has convinced me of his more than occasional usefulness. But he came to my attention early in the war, and when I first, of necessity, began to keep confidential files of his movements, he was *Gentian* in the cipher.'

" 'Who was *Predecessor?*' I said.

" 'A woman,' he said. 'I never met her, and I never took the trouble to inquire of her name. There were dangers in too much knowledge, then.'

" 'What were they doing?' I said.

"He showed a great deal of hesitancy before he replied," Andrew said, "something I had not seen until after our first discussion, and the use I made of it, had persuaded him that I was to be trusted.

" 'It's so long ago,' he said. 'Most are dead, and I suppose the rest soon will be. Still, I embarked upon this at first because Cable requested it. Requested my help. I would want no desecration of his memory.'

" 'I know that,' I said. 'There won't be any.'

"He waited some more," Andrew said. " 'Cable was not a temperate man, in some few things,' he said. 'I do not mean that he overindulged himself. I mean that when he had concluded that his cause was just, he was single-minded and ferocious in its pursuits. He did nothing that was illegal, but he facilitated the acts of others which verged upon illegality, believing passionately that the better ends were served thereby.

" 'In time of war,' he said, 'that sort of man can be of inestimable utility to his country, because he will find a way to do things when the circumstances are urgently exigent, without regard for the cost to himself. He had learned enough in the Office of the Coordinator of Information, before the war actually began, to persuade him to very firm views. He was disposed to act upon them.

" 'That,' he said, 'and you will, I am sure, find this incredible, is all that I really know. I did not inquire into his activities, because I was not involved in their inceptions or their management, and there was no need to know. I was merely the go-between, the messenger, as it were.'

" 'For whom?' I said.

" 'That much, I am afraid,' he said, 'I will have to keep to myself. When my principal desired a conference with Cable, I arranged it. I do not know what they discussed, or what occurred as a result. My duties, in respect to that operation, were to act as a clearinghouse for changes in location, so that I would always be able to reach them, immediately. This, I did.'

" 'What was Wills' material filed under?' I said.

" '*Northside*,' he said.

" 'But you don't know what they were up to?' I said.

" 'Andrew,' he said, 'I don't even know the code name for the operation. I never did.'

"Miss Springer came in again, about then," Andrew said. "Miss Springer said that Mister Morgan would be in transit from Hong Kong until the middle of September. After that, he would be in winter quarters. He smiled: 'It's futile to pursue Henry when he's traveling,' he said. 'I suggest you wait until he lights. *Winter quarters* is Virgin Gorda.'

" 'Will he see me there?' I said.

" 'I can arrange it,' he said.

" I may ask you to,' I said. And I left.

"The first thing I did," Andrew said, "was call Gammage. And: start bluffing. 'Okay,' I said, 'I'm part of the way, anyway. I've got *Gentian* pegged, and I'm pretty well on the way to *Predecessor*.'

" 'Not enough,' he croaked at me.

" 'I've also got *Northside*,' I said. 'And I think I know where to find *Gentian* in a while, and start asking him some questions.'

" 'Very good,' he said. 'Then you will require no further assistance from me.'

" 'Very true,' I said. 'But, of course, if I don't get it, you won't be allowed your review of what I write.'

"Now I had him," Andrew said. " 'What do you want?' he said. 'I want to go into this thing prepared for it,' I said. 'I want to know everything I possibly can, in advance, code names, specific plans, everything.'

"He began to laugh," Andrew said. "I had lost him again.

'Mister Collier,' he said with great patience, 'I know youth is impatient, but your imagination has truly run off with you. *Gentian* can tell you a great deal. But most of it is very harmless, devoid of the swashbuckling that I'm sure you would desire. This was an undertaking in the real world, where the acquisition of information is what carries most importance.

"In conflict, what is significant is prior knowledge of what your enemy contemplates, so that you can take affirmative or negative action. Not to prevent him from doing it, but to prevent him from gaining any benefit from doing it. If you should see me preparing to throw a right cross, early enough, you would sensibly take your chin out of range. A little later, and you would be forced to accept the blow on your glove. Later still, on the forearm. And, too late, upon your chin. But you cannot prevent me from attempting the punch. If you are wise, you will seek only to avoid it, and to position yourself to deliver a counterblow when I have unbalanced myself.

" 'Mister Collier,' he said, wheezing and gasping, 'we had no cloaks, and very few daggers. We had companies, and couriers, and contacts and the knowledge, to begin with, of what we were looking for. That was all there was. And it was not information about troop movements, or planned attacks, or diagrams of defensive fortifications. That was the responsibility of others.'

Andrew stopped now, the ice clinking in his empty glass. "Do you remember," he said to me, "what used to happen every year, when the snow melted away around the house in Milton, and your mother went out to tend the flowers?"

"Of course I remember," I said. "It killed her, in the end."

"Well," he said, "there were some she didn't have to tend, weren't there?

"Didn't have to," he said, "and didn't want to. There was only one person in the house who gave a shit about those flowers, and I remember he used to yell at the gardener for cutting them when he did the lawn."

"The violets," I said. "The violets on the shady side of the house. Sure."

" 'When God gives you something for nothing,' he said," Andrew said, " 'don't go and kill it. Appreciate it. And protect it.'

" 'What others?' I said to Gammage. 'Why,' he said, 'the others in the organization.'

" 'What was the name for it?' I asked.

" 'For whatever difference it makes,' he said, 'it was *Operation Violet.*' "

"So, what do you do now, Andrew?" Ellen said.

"I've already done the first thing," Andrew said. "I've gotten Priddy's okay. It was like laying a square egg, but I've got it. I'm going to see Morgan."

"I don't envy you," I said.

"You don't need to," Andrew said, "since you're coming with me."

Ellen and I spoke together. "*Why?*"

Andrew's voice was calm in the darkness. "Because this guy's gonna maybe try and blow a whole lotta smoke up my ass, about closed corporations and international trade, and shit like that."

"I know very little about that, Andrew," I said.

He spoke in that silky way he has. "Morgan doesn't know that," he said. "All Morgan's gonna know is that you're Cable Wills' son, and a partner in the old firm, and that alone'll make him cautious."

"I can't go down there," I said.

"Daniel," he said, "you're coming."

X

I DO NOT BELIEVE in acting hastily. But neither has my experience shown me any reason to believe that difficult tasks are eased in their completion by procrastination. We take pride, at Wills, Cable, in the expeditious resolution of our client's problems, frequently to the consternation of opposing counsel who consider that two or three years of delay between the opening and the closing of a file is no more than appropriate.

For most of us, that habit of promptitude carries over into the conduct of our personal business. By the end of January 1972, less than two weeks after Dad's death, I had arranged a conference with Larry Cable, who handles not only the probate side of our practice, but also the probate matters of members of the firm who request him to plan their estates. When Harrison Cable passed away, Larry had succeeded to, among others, the management and oversight of my father's estate. I had utter confidence in him, and I told him that I would rely entirely upon his judgment in my duties as executor of Dad's estate.

He nodded. "I should think it would proceed smoothly enough," he said. "I've reviewed the file, of course, since Cable passed away, and I find that we were able to dispense with our annual review this past year; there's a note that I spoke to Cable, and he said that neither his circumstances nor his sentiments had altered, so that matters could stand as they were."

Now Larry bent to the file before him. He is rather farsighted, but inclined to leave his glasses wherever he puts them when someone interrupts his reading, and then to suffer along without them until he runs across them again. "There is the usual A trust," he said. "You, Ellen and the boys are the beneficiaries, of course. You, I and Old Colony are the trustees. Five years after his death, five years from now, that is, there is a power to invade principal, upon vote of the majority of the trustees." He looked up. "I should anticipate no difficulty from that," he said.

"None," I said. "Can you approximate the corpus?"

"I can do somewhat better than that," he said. "I had Mrs. Bogner check with the Old Colony, and the corpus, consisting of stocks, bonds, and some convertible debentures, has a current market value of approximately seventy thousand dollars. The annual yield, for the past year, was in dividends and appreciation, on the order of six thousand, five hundred dollars. This, of course, is primarily the corpus of the marital deduction trust, which we converted into an A trust at your mother's death."

"Of course," I said.

"Then there is a *B* trust," Larry said. "The *B* trust was established when your son Hadley was born, with an initial funding of twenty thousand dollars. It was amended upon the birth of your son Lee, to add him as a beneficiary, and another ten thousand dollars was added to the corpus. This is expressly stated to be for the purposes of financing their education." Larry shook his head. He looked up again, somewhat troubled in his expression. "Cable directed us to see to the investment of those monies in certain mutual funds, about fourteen years ago. We had no especial prejudice against mutual funds, of course, but lacked confidence in particular ones that he had chosen. He could not be dissuaded, even when reminded of the difficulties of liquidating such investments. There was no breach of fiduciary duty, of course, since Cable himself was one of the trustees, with you to succeed him. But several of those funds were not on the approved list, and we thought them very speculative. Now, as you *have* succeeded him, I think we ought to get together very soon, and sell off some of the dogs, take whatever losses have accrued, and retrench into safer positions."

I was, as you may imagine, very much concerned. "What is the current value of the corpus?"

"Happily," Larry said, "the funds which we recommended have performed very well indeed. Half of the funding was invested in them, a total of fifteen thousand dollars, and the shares thus acquired have a current market value in excess of forty-three thousand dollars, with an average seven- to eight-percent yield.

"Shares purchased with ten thousand dollars of what Cable liked to call his venture capital cannot be realistically assessed now at more than two or three thousand dollars, and there is no active market in them.

"The remaining five thousand dollars of his venture capital went into a fund specializing in the acquisition of oil exploration rights in Alaska, and their current value is so speculative as to cause me to advise you that, rather than part with them for pennies, we may as well hold onto them. There will be an amount, obviously, at least substantially offsetting the educational expenses of the boys, but it currently appears that it will not suffice, that principal will have to be invaded, and that Cable's decision, enforced upon the rest of us, prevented the establishment of a fund which would now be worth in excess of eighty-five thousand dollars." He shook his head.

"My most difficult clients, I find," he said, "are the ones who practice law with me."

In 1974, Dad's thousand shares of Consolidated Alaska Drilling Fund reacted to approval of the Trans-Alaskan Pipeline project, and we trustees unanimously voted to sell them at the market value of fifty-three dollars a share. Later they went to seventy, and a little beyond, but we had no regrets.

"There is a *C* trust," Larry said, "established when you and Ellen were married. Cable funded it with fifteen thousand dollars and directed that the trustees invest it, and reinvest profits, until your death, if you should predecease her, the corpus then to be paid over to her, or upon her death, if she should predecease you, paid over to you. It's worth a little over twenty-eight thousand dollars now.

"There is a *D* trust," Larry said. "The corpus was ten thousand dollars. The beneficiary is Andrew Collier. He is to receive the income until he attains the age of sixty-five years, and then the principal. He has a power to appoint until then, of course.

"There are a number of specific bequests," Larry said. "The College, the church, minor bequests of one or two thousand dollars to people in the firm. Then there is the provision for disposition of the contents of his safety-deposit box, personal articles and so forth, and for automobiles, household furnishings. With the exception of articles otherwise labeled in the safety-deposit box, all of that goes to you. There is provision for the boat: that is to go to Andrew Collier."

I knew Larry was studying me from under his eyebrows, which are black and coarse. Not to determine whether I was as surprised as he expected, but to determine whether I had expected such a development.

In fact, I had. I would have been more surprised if there had not been such a provision, or one equivalent to it.

I had objected, as strenuously as filial respect permitted, to the decision to sell the house in Duxbury. It was not because I disliked Nantucket, which is very beautiful. But I had grown up in Duxbury, and I was fond of it. Each year after we were married, Ellen and I would move there with our children, as I had planned it, and I had counted on giving to them the same memories that I cherished. When Dad informed me, the day we spent together in Milton, watching the inauguration of John F. Kennedy, that he had put the Duxbury house on the market, I was dismayed, and I guess it showed.

"Your reasons are selfish," he said, without any hint of rancor. "For you and Ellen, Duxbury would be preferable, still. But you drive, Compton, and I do not. And you must continue to visit the office each day, for most of the summer, whereas I am an elder statesman now, and need only come to the city once or twice between Memorial Day and Labor Day. It is time for me to begin to conserve my energies. And besides, I wish to. So, I am being selfish also, but I am being selfish with what is mine to be selfish with, and that, like taking the road less traveled by, makes all the difference."

He had never confided in me the details of the transactions, the sale of the Duxbury place and the purchase of the house at

Monomoy, and I, of course, never looked them up. We made a compromise of things: Ellen, at first when he moved to the island in the spring, then after the boys were born and in school, when the schools closed in June, moved down there, and I batched it in Lincoln during the week, driving down to Woods Hole for the Friday night ferry and returning Monday mornings. I took three weeks in August with all, and it was pleasant, but I confess that I was lonely again.

"There is," Larry said now, "no direct devise of the realty on Nantucket." Again he studied me, this time openly. "Have you any idea of its value?"

"No accurate one," I said. "It's a large house, about twelve rooms, in a very desirable area. And it's nicely furnished. There are water rights. I never asked him, but from the local papers, and what little opportunity I had to read them, I should say it must be worth somewhere in the neighborhood of a hundred and fifty to a hundred and sixty thousand dollars. Today. Of course, I don't know whether he mortgaged it, or the amount of the mortgage."

"Um," Larry said. "Well, these figures are not precise, but they are good enough to work with. As best we can determine, the sale of the Duxbury house brought about fifty thousand dollars, which Cable immediately used as the first payment on the Nantucket house.

"Now," he said, "we are in somewhat deeper waters. Cable was sixty-two, then, and apparently either did not seek bank financing — for fear that his advanced age would be reason for it to be denied to him — or sought it, and was refused. The transaction was accomplished without a broker — Cable negotiated the purchase himself, with the heirs of the previous owner — so there is no help there, and he took the precaution of affixing more revenue stamps than necessary to the deed that he recorded. If those stamps were employed as the index, he paid in excess of two hundred and thirty thousand dollars for the house, which is plainly ridiculous. According to our people there, the actual price was probably somewhere in the neighborhood of a hundred and ten thousand dollars."

"Leaving," I said, "about sixty thousand dollars that he got from somewhere else."

"Exactly," Larry said. "Now keep that in mind. In nineteen seventy, Cable executed a codicil to this will, removing the Nantucket house from the residue of the estate, and assigning it as collateral to the Bass River Savings Bank, for a personal loan in the face amount of seventy-five thousand dollars, which amount, with interest accrued thereon at the rate of six percent per annum, unless sooner discharged, shall be paid from the proceeds of the sale of the house, and the balance thereof shall pass into the residue of the estate.

"He made some interest payments," Larry said, "but not many. The balance of the loan is about eighty-four thousand dollars, and the bank wants its money. But this is a very poor time of the year to sell a house on Nantucket, and as his executors, we should consider whether we are authorized to *cy pres* this instrument, paying off the loan from other assets and retaining the property for sale in the spring."

"All right," I said.

"Unless, of course," Larry said, "you wanted to keep the place."

"I don't," I said.

"The house in Milton," Larry said, "passes outside the will, unless you should have predeceased him. As you recall, he had you named joint tenant with him, after your mother died. But, for estate tax purposes, have you any idea of its approximate value?"

"It must be large," I said. "I don't know, somewhere in the neighborhood of two hundred thousand dollars?"

"A little more than that, actually," Larry said. "Now, the next clause deals with stocks, bonds, cash or money on hand, that sort of thing. The last time we talked, he had very little of any of that. I believe he had about twenty thousand dollars, which he used to dabble in the stock market. He held all his stocks jointly with you, so there will be no difficulty in liquidating them. His savings, the last time we reviewed his affairs, came to about thirty thousand dollars more. And that's about it."

"What about insurance?" I said.

"Ahh," Larry said, "against my father's advice, your Dad years ago opted to drop all of his twenty-payment life and straight-life insurance, in favor of Bar Association term insurance. His reasoning was that he could obtain much more coverage — I think it was a total of a hundred and fifty thousand dollars or so — for the same money, and of course that was true. But it all was reduced to a total of about fifteen thousand dollars, as soon as he reached sixty-five. There is some, but not much."

I admit that I was distressed, but not yet disheartened. That still left his interest in the firm.

Different firms handle partnership interests differently. Carson Wills and Harrison Cable had struck an even bargain, beginning each with a fifty percent share of profits. As new partners were admitted to the firm, each of them ceded an equal number of percentage points to the new partner. Sometimes they allowed established lawyers to buy into the firm, selling points, as they are now known, at prices which varied with the times. Associates rising to partnership were awarded points, and allowed, sometimes, to purchase additional ones. Commonly, the addition of the new partner meant that while the share of revenue went down, the revenue to be shared was substantially increased, so that, for example, a thirty-five per-

cent share of Wills, Cable, profits in 1935 was worth more, substantially more, than a fifty percent share in 1918. Mark
Dunnigan, for example, was admitted to partnership with two
and one-half points, in 1965, and promptly elected to exercise
the option simultaneously proffered: to purchase an additional
three and one-half points from the estate of Harrison Cable,
for seventy thousand dollars.

"He had none," Larry said. And now he was looking me
straight in the face. I tried to speak, and I could not. I tried
again, and still could not.

Admitted to partnership in 1966, with one and one-half
points, I had secured new business and performed old, well
enough to be granted an addition of one and three-quarter
points, by 1972. Until we moved to the new building, over my
objections, my three and one-quarter percent share, over and
above my draw of eighteen hundred dollars a month, had
brought me around thirty thousand dollars a year. The overhead at 28 State Street — the firm moved to the new building
in 1971 — diminished that by about two thousand dollars a
year. Having no idea at all of what my father's interest in the
firm had been, I had in my pessimistic moments calculated it
at no less than six to eight percent, and in optimistic ones, as
high as twelve percent. In either mood, I routinely declined
opportunities to purchase interests of partners deceased, leaving for the bench, or retiring, believing that my principal leg-
acy from my father would be his interest in Wills, Cable.

"Compton," Larry said, "I was afraid you did not know.
He assured my father that he'd told you, and then that he
would tell you, and he told me that he had told you. Ahh," he
said, leaning back and throwing his pencil on the desk, shaking
his head: "I really must insist on farming this work out." He
rubbed his tired eyes and arose from his chair. With his back
to me, as though he had been too courteous to look me in the

eye, he said: "They were a hardworking, self-disciplined, self-sacrificing generation of individualists, Carson and my father. They started this from nothing, made a few mistakes, cut their losses ruthlessly, drove themselves unmercifully, first built prestigious reputations, then improved upon them."

He turned to me. "They provided for their families," he said. "When they drank, it was in such moderation that it was barely drinking at all. When they married, they stayed married. They were strict, and the demands they placed on their employees were no less punishing than the ones that they observed for themselves, but seldom as severe. They populated the bench and they ran their town governments. They were as diligent as beavers, as determined as badgers" (Larry is an ardent naturalist) "and as secretive as voles. And that is invariably where the damage was done."

Larry sat down again. He rested his elbows on his desk, and cupped his chin in his hands. He stared directly at me. "I was given to understand that you had heard this from one of the people who was involved," he said. "Since you have not, and the others are dead and gone, you will have to hear it from me. And I was not there.

"What was evidently your expectation this morning was, until right after World War Two, the standing policy of the firm: upon second-generation partners of the firm devolved the partnership interest of the first-generation partner, at his death, retirement, or formal declaration. Unless he chose to dispose of it otherwise. That was the partner's individual decision, to be made in his own, complete discretion; the only limitation on it was that his share could not be offered outside the firm. Only to other than existing partners, pro rata, or to the treasury of the firm, which of course had the effect of retiring some shares and, for the time being, increasing the value of outstanding shares.

"When Cable joined the firm," Larry said, "your grandfather's share was in the neighborhood of forty percent, and so was my father's. People worked for much less money in those days, and that was a good thing, because there was much less money around. But the firm expanded rapidly in the twenties and the thirties, and its ability to respond effectively to new business demanded the infusion of personnel with some fair amount of experience. So, while the revenues increased remarkably, they did so at the expense of partnership shares retained by the founders.

"When Cable was admitted to partnership in nineteen thirty," Larry said, "he was voted five points, even by the standards of those years an extraordinarily generous provision for a new man. From what I can tell, that share was worth about ten or twelve thousand dollars, a substantial amount of money in those days. 'And it was not,' my father told me, when something I said evidently prompted him to think that I considered myself to have been less munificently treated, 'because he was Carson's son. In those days, being the son of the founding partner would have brought the same consideration it brought you. It was because he brought business. Before he went bad, Cable Wills was . . .'"

I was even more dumbfounded, if that had been possible. Larry saw my face collapse, of course. "Shit," he said. He got up again. He turned his back to me, to give me a chance to compose myself. His voice was strained, when he resumed. "I assume, Compton," he said, "that you understand how much I regret that unfortunate remark."

I said that I did. He still did not look at me, but faced out into the sunlight over Boston. "Personally, I think," he said, "I could've understood it, and probably did. As much as anyone here did. That was at the root of their reaction: they did not understand.

"As I got to know him," Larry said, "I began to understand

that Cable required a great deal of latitude, much more than anyone else here had, or was permitted. And it puzzled me. His work was much less subject to review and supervision; as you know, notwithstanding our specialization, we circulate files regularly among the partners, so as to be sure that no aspect of a case has been overlooked. He neither solicited nor expected such oversight, nor did he tolerate it when it happened. He was out of town a lot. Until I was admitted to partnership, indeed, and commenced gradually to succeed to my father's management position, I could think only that Cable had somehow intimidated the other partners to the point at which they permitted him to do as he wished. Such men can be useful to a law firm.

"Then," he said, "it was around nineteen forty-eight, nineteen forty-nine, I've forgotten, now, exactly when, my father started turning over to me the day-to-day operation of the firm, I found myself thoroughly unable to master the arcane system of accounts that we employed. One partner drew one amount; another drew twice that, but only half as often; two had independent means and took their entire shares at the end of the year; two had no means, and drew one-fourth the base monthly amount, once a week; your father drew nothing at all. It was chaos.

"I couldn't make head nor tail of it," Larry said. "I went to my father, having no wish to disrupt the orderly business of the firm, and asked him, please, to explain things to me. Commencing with the agreement that matters had to be regularized, if for no other reason than to reduce the amount of money spent on bookkeeping, we went down the list, establishing a regular monthly draw, and determining to do the best we could to persuade the other partners to institute our proposal at the next partnership meeting. That brought us to Cable.

" 'Cable draws nothing at all,' I said.

" 'That's as it should be,' Dad said.

" 'But he's a partner,' I said.

" 'In name only,' Dad said. 'He has no partnership share.'

" 'His father was a founder,' I said.

" 'He was,' my father said, 'and Carson had a substantial share. But it was a share of profits from this business, from year to year, produced, in part, from his work. When he died, in nineteen forty-four, he did no further work.'

" 'But Cable?' I said.

" 'Cable elected to take another route,' he said. 'He became inflamed with another purpose. His choice was to continue at his purpose, to the detriment of the business. We did not, of course, prohibit him from doing so, if that was his choice. But, after several years of his interests interfering with those of the firm, we were obliged to deny to him for the following year the share of firm income which he had not increased, but diminished. He protested that it was his father's share, and pursuant to the articles of agreement, which we drew up when the firm became larger, we invoked our option to buy him out.'

" 'We bought him out, I think it was, in nineteen fifty. He has since received credit for all business which he has brought in to the firm and for all work that he has done for the firm, and nothing more. My sentiments were to reduce him to *Of Counsel* on the letterhead, but they were not followed.'

" 'But what has he done?' I said.

" 'In several particulars,' Dad said, 'I neither know nor wish to know. What he has undertaken for the firm, he has done well. And if you will consult the files, you will find that his annual credited share of profits has afforded him a very comfortable income. What else he has done, is his business.'

"That," Larry said, "is really all that I can tell you. Cable's points went back into treasury, and he received somewhere in the neighborhood of a hundred thousand dollars."

"What would that be worth today?" I said.

"Let me think," Larry said, "inflation and all, allowing for reduction in points but for increase in billings, oh, perhaps four hundred thousand dollars."

With Larry's help, and Simon Rosen's in our tax department, I was able to reduce the combined federal and state tax levy on Dad's estate to the modest sum of two hundred and fifty-three thousand dollars. That, after the Bass River Savings Bank was satisfied, left the various trusts, Andrew's boat, the house in Monomoy, and the personal articles. The bulk of the taxes were met from the proceeds of the sale of the house in Milton. The furniture brought almost nothing.

In July of 1973, I sold the house at Monomoy for one hundred and sixty thousand dollars, furnished. Ellen and the boys were upset, but I was adamant: we have rented, since then, at Chatham, and the proceeds of that sale are in reliable investments.

XI

Even on a comparatively large boat, as *African Violet* is, there is relatively little privacy. As Andrew is fond of saying: "She'll fuck twelve, sleep six, and fight four. And you sure-God better be good friends when you get on, because if you're not, you're gonna be sworn enemies when you get off."

After the exchange in the cockpit at Eel Pond that night, there seemed nothing more of general interest to discuss. The women went below, Deirdre pausing behind Ellen on the companionway steps to look back toward Andrew and say: "It'd be okay if you helped too, you know."

"I know that," Andrew said, "and I know something else,

too: it'll be all right if I don't." That left, I thought, three of the four people aboard annoyed at one another; as it turned out, I was off by one.

We ate the Stroganoff and the bread, and drank the wine, in the cockpit. When we finished, it was ten-thirty, and Andrew made it clear that he wanted a nightcap. I did not, and followed the women below. To Deirdre, I said: "Andrew wants another Jim Beam."

Now I did not consider that a particularly provocative remark. But evidently it was. "Let him get it himself, the fucker," she said.

I was taken aback. I guess that I must have looked inquiringly at Ellen. "I agree with her," she said. "Or maybe you'd prefer to get it for him." I did so, and joined him with one of my own. We sat in silence in the cockpit until the clashing of pans and dishes had ended in the galley. It was around eleven.

Deirdre came up the companionway again. Looking directly at me, she said: "Ellen's going to bed."

I was ready for that myself. I said that I would go below, and I did, leaving them in the cockpit to settle their own differences.

Ellen was changing in the forward cabin, where Andrew and Deirdre would sleep. I pulled off my windbreaker, shirt, pants and Topsiders, and climbed into my bunk. When she came out, I was wrapped up. "Come in here," she whispered, fiercely.

She meant the forward cabin. I got up and followed her in.

"What has he got on you?" she said.

"Nothing," I said.

"Then why're you going?" she said. "You're the man who won't take a ferry without complaining, and now you're going to fly to the West Indies, because somebody you don't like very much, tells you, you have to?"

Flying terrifies me, and she knows it. There is in fact no variety of travel that I really enjoy, except trains, and I can't enjoy them anymore, either. Ellen, of course, knows this: when we were married, we took a Mooremack from New York to Bermuda, and I spent most of the passage choking back seasickness. But flying distresses me even more. I am sure it's attributable to the same malfunctions of the inner ear that make me uncomfortable on the water.

"It doesn't make sense, Comp," she said. "Come on, what is it? If you can't tell me, who the hell can you tell? I am your wife, after all, although it doesn't seem to matter to you more than five or six times a year. Is it another woman? Have you got another woman, that he knows about?"

I chose to ignore that. "I suppose it's curiosity," I said. "I'm curious, as much as anything else. I thought I knew this man who was my father. Then I started finding out there were so many things I didn't know about him, and many that I still don't understand."

That day in his office, Larry Cable said to me, as we concluded our discussion: "Don't feel any worse'n you have to, Comp. He was an enigma to my father, and something of a conundrum to Carson, too. And they were better off than the rest. *They* didn't understand him at all."

"I suppose," I said to Ellen in the forward cabin, "I'm simply curious."

I had never seen her look at me like that before. "I guess you must be," she said. "You're certainly yellow." She alluded to the Swedish movie. Then she opened the way to the main cabin, stalked out and clambered into her bunk.

I was too tired to protest. I got into my bunk, also, pulled up the covers and put out the light. There were a few stars visible through the open hatch.

For a long time there was no sound from the cockpit. At length Ellen began to breathe in a light and regular snore, and I suppose they must have assumed that we were both asleep. Or, in the alternative, that if either was awake, they could not be heard.

"All right, Andrew," Deirdre said, in a very hostile whisper, "what the fuck is going *on* between you two?"

"We're taking a trip," Andrew whispered hoarsely, "to find some things out."

"It's more than that, Andrew," she said. "You're *awful* to him. You're an absolute *prick* to him. And he's scared of you, Andrew. Why is he scared of you?"

"Maybe he's scared of what I'm going to find out about his father," Andrew said. "Maybe he's scared that I'm not going to find out. I really don't know. I don't much give a shit. If he's scared that I'm not gonna find out, his fears're groundless and I'll soon take care of them. If he's scared I'm gonna find out, it's not gonna do him any good, because I'm gonna find out. Maybe he wants to find out, himself. The old bastard *was* kind of a puzzle. He looked like he was one thing, but he almost always did the other."

"Does that give you a license to torment his son?" she said.

"You know," Andrew said, "the night that I got old enough to stay out late, there was a woman up and glaring at me when I finally got home. That went on till I moved out of the house. Then, for a long time, I stayed out late and I did what I liked, and came home at all hours, and there wasn't anybody glaring at me. So, I got lulled into a false sense of security, I guess. I met this woman, and when I was seeing her, I got home very late indeed, and nobody was there glaring at me. Some nights, in fact, I didn't get home at all, and there was still nobody glaring at me. So I got married."

"Andrew," she said, warningly.

"Well," he said, "that was not one of my better ideas. Oh, it was all right when I was on the road, because she managed to find something to occupy her time. But when I was due home, she stayed home, especially for me, and when I got home late, there she was, glaring at me. I used to take this a lot harder, before I found out why she was so sure I'd caused her to waste an evening. If she'd've known I was coming home late, she could've gone out and come in just a little earlier, and then she would've been nowhere near as pissed off."

"Andrew," she said again.

"So," he said, "I got divorced. And I tried to think where I went wrong. And I did what old Mahoney at the next desk used to say he was doing, when his head hurt so bad from cheap booze that he couldn't lift it up and hadda sit with it on the desk all day, while the rest of us covered for him: I made an examination of conscience. And what I decided was, I'd been asking too much of women, and not delivering enough."

"You were half right," she said.

"See?" he said. "That actually improves my average, would you believe it? I resolved, then and there, that I was gonna listen more, and talk less, whenever I was talking to a woman. I was gonna find out what the women wanted, and I was gonna tell 'em what I wanted, and we were gonna be *equals.* Right?"

"Where did you go wrong?" she said.

"I wished I knew," he said. "It always started off all right. I would meet this woman for the first time, and sooner or later she would make it clear that she wanted to know what I was after.

"Now," he said, "what I learned is this: there generally ain't no right answer to that question. If I was after her pants, and I told the truth, she either liked the idea or she didn't. If she liked it, she said she didn't, or I was too impetuous. If she didn't like it, she told me so, in no uncertain terms. And if I wasn't, and I said so, it was even worse. So I got smart. I figured out, when that question's hanging in the air, you pick the answer that you think she'll like, and you give that."

"And what happens then?" she said.

"You will always be wrong," he said. "Because, as I said, there ain't no right answer to that question. If you don't want to, you're a faggot, and if you do, you're a rapist, and probably a pedophile too.

"That," Andrew said, "was when I started to get some sense. I decided, after a few turns of that carousel, that what a woman basically is, is contrary, and the best thing to do is lay the absolute goddamned truth on her and let her dislike that, because it's easier to keep track of later, and it don't require as much effort to think it up."

"You son of a bitch," she said.

"That's probably about right," he said. "See, I see all these liberated women. And on the first night they always tell me they had it sewn up, and anyway, they got lots of boyfriends. 'Okay,' I say. 'I got laid about ten, eleven years ago, ended the suspense. We gonna have din-din or not?'

"By dessert," Andrew said, "they're inquiring about all my other girlfriends. Not just name, rank and serial number, either. I don't answer. I wouldn't give out that information if there was any to give out."

"Bullshit," she said.

"Precisely what you got, when you started in on that canticle, just like all the rest, and I wouldn't answer you, either," Andrew said. "Now, from all of that, in turn, I got another proposition, which I adhere to like it was the lodestone: you're here because I want you to be, and because you want to be. Both things. Batteries wired in series. One fails, they all go out."

"I think you're crazy," she said, "and mean, too."

"Well," he said, "Deirdre, that's the point of the parable, and the gist of it, too. You're a very quick study. You see, I don't give a shit what you think."

I believe I gave a convincing appearance of being asleep as she came stomping down the companionway. When he did, if he did, I missed it, because I was in fact asleep.

XII

LITERALLY shivering with fear from the flight, in the warm, hushed evening, I got out of the battered green van after Andrew, who was, I think, somewhat shaken himself. We stood on the concrete dock as the massive black driver placed our grips next to us. We had reached the inlet by a mountain road no more than one and one-half cars wide, crowded in farther by landslides that had left boulders and small uprooted trees on the rutted surfaces. In places the road had washed out, and been indifferently repaired. In others, goats danced across in front of us, and the driver had taken hairpin turns and switchbacks as though completely assured that nothing would be coming in the opposite direction. At times at least a thousand feet above the seas glowing in the last of the afternoon light, I had tried to avoid looking over the unprotected side of the road, down the sheer cliffs to the rocks.

Evidently working according to other arrangements, the driver appeared to ignore Andrew's offer of payment. Without saying anything, he climbed back into his van, backed it around, and left us in the evening on the dock, by ourselves. Forty feet away, beached on a mud flat, was a derelict motor cruiser, sheared off just behind the cabinhouse, its ragged hull planking rotting away. There were three small gray dories, with outboards attached, moored to tall poles sunk into the bottom, and the steep mountainsides climbed around us and hemmed us in. The raucous exhaust sound of the van died away.

From a headland, around to our right, we began to hear the sound of a large outboard motor. As it grew louder, we heard also the pounding of a hull planing on a moderate chop. Then a Boston Whaler, about twenty feet long, swung out wide around the headland, pointed in toward where we stood, and began to drop in the water.

"Good enough," Andrew said. "Unless this is the guy that takes us to the guy that cuts off an ear and sends it home with the ransom note."

The black man at the wheel brought the Whaler in precisely to the side of the dock, stepped from the controls, disregarded Andrew's hand, outstretched to take a line, and held the boat against the pilings with his hands. He had very thick forearms. When he was satisfied that he had things under control, he gestured toward our grips. We brought them over and he took each of them and placed them in the boat. He had some difficulty with Dad's valise; the handle had been damaged, several years ago, and pinched the fingers of the uninitiated. Without complaining, though, he indicated that we were to come aboard and sit on the cushioned bench behind the control panel. We did so, and he handed the boat away from the dock, backed it perilously close to where the derelict lay aground, and took it out toward the headland, at immediate full throttle.

We left a broad shining wake in the sunset light that came around the headland to port, as we turned the headland to starboard with most of the hull out of the water. Headed east, now, we saw large sailboats lighted at their moorings in an inlet off to the north, and others coming in, single file, through what was evidently a channel to the west, but a narrow one. Conversation was impossible, over the roar of the motor.

Behind the headland that we turned was a series of three more. We turned to starboard at the third one and the black man abruptly cut the power. The boat settled down into the water and approached slowly a small wooden dock built out from a beach no more than fifty feet long and fifteen feet wide. On the dock there were two black women. There was no sign of a house or a light. A large pelican flew in over the headland to our starboard, evidently spotted something among the roots of the trees exposed at the water's edge, and plummeted in for his dinner.

The black man handed the boat along the dock and went forward. He passed our grips onto the dock. Then he came aft and indicated that we were to get out. We did as he wished. Still without any attempt at conversation, he handed the Whaler out again, backed it, and stood it on its transom again. Before we could collect ourselves, the women had picked up our grips and started down the dock with them. We followed.

At the end of the dock, grayish-green in the gray evening against the green hills, there was a Volkswagen Thing, a small four-passenger open car with a canvas roof. As the women approached it, the black man at the wheel started the engine and switched on the lights. The women put the bags in the front seat with him. It was plain that we were expected to get in the back, and we did so.

The black man backed the vehicle around and drove across the sand to a large stand of bushes that were covered with red flowers. He made a hard left and we were on a dirt road.

At times it seemed that we were on a seventy percent grade, even though the narrow road doubled back and forth up the side of the rocky mountainside, closed in at times by the large flowering bushes, at others cramped by tall strands of cactus and outcroppings of rock. Negotiating the switchback turns, the hood of the car pointed to the sky.

We emerged at last into a broad clearing, where a house, in darkness until our headlights hit it, was laid in against the mountainside, its view to the north where the sailing boats swung at their anchors. At once, the house was illuminated from within, and small lights, shaded by large black discs, threw light on the path to the house.

The black man parked the vehicle. By now we were better able to perceive what was expected of us. We got out and started up the path. Small lizards, chameleons, perhaps, skittered away from our approach.

On the verandah there was an enormous black woman in a green and white gingham dress and a white apron and a white, starched cap. Bowing to us, she indicated that we should follow. Behind us, the black man brought our bags.

We were shown through a foyer floored with a red tile, furnished with a heavy, black credenza of what appeared to be Moorish design. Overhead there was an octagonal black lantern suspended from a chain. There was a large mirror, which gave us an adequate, though brief, confirmation of our dishevelment. We went on through a dining salon, also floored in the red tile, and also furnished with heavy black furniture. Candles burned in golden sconces. Turning to our right, we passed through an opulently done sitting room, mostly in beige and gold, and came to a flight of stairs. At the top of the stairs we were shown into our bedroom, large, with oversized double beds and a view through open wooden jalousies of the anchorage to the north. The adjoining bath was luxurious.

The black man entered with our grips. The woman, as the black man began to unpack our things, looked at us inquiringly.

Andrew said: "Even before I clean up, I think we could use a drink."

She smiled professionally at that, and led us back down the stairs. Proceeding straight through the living area this time, we came to a library, well stocked, and a set of sliding screen doors leading onto the same verandah that we had found at the end of the path. There mosquito candles burned, and low wicker chairs with thick cushions of green and yellow were grouped around small white metal tables. We chose the table in the center and sat down, to study the view in the evening. The black woman went to a wet bar and we heard ice and glasses brought together. "You know," Andrew said, "the only reason I don't stand on my rights and *demand* a goddamned bourbon is because I'm beginning to think I'll do better in this place if I just keep my mouth shut. Isn't this something?"

"Paradise," I said. "You sure we didn't in fact die on that ride, and that's really where we are?"

"Not at all," Andrew said. The place had its effect on us. Uncertain whether the staff spoke English, we conversed softly, as though not to offend them with the sounds of an alien language. "I haven't seen anything like this since I covered the Monte Carlo Rallye in seventy-one."

The black woman returned then, with tall glasses, which she placed on the table before us. We drank, gratefully. It was a heavy, sweet rum, and ginger ale, and it was wonderful. Andrew and I smiled appreciatively, and nodded to her.

She nodded, first, in reply, really, that bow she had. Then she said, in perfect though accented English: "The master must rest now, each day, but he will be down shortly. I have left ice, and other beverages if you prefer them, at the bar. Please help yourself." Then she was gone.

I suppose we waited there, fully content, by ourselves, for a little less than an hour. Andrew made the second round, and I the third. While I was at the bar, one of the black women who had met us at the dock, now in the green and white gingham uniform, came onto the verandah with a large tray of an excellent spinach quiche. From the channel to the west, a very large sailing vessel, brilliantly lighted and white in her own light against the indigo sky and water, entered the sheltered harbor, too far from us for the sound of her engine to carry. "You know something?" Andrew said, after a very long silence, "I *know* I'm getting softened up, and for once I don't even give a shit. I've been softened up by the best of them, and it's never worked, that I know of. But this time, it might. It just might. If Priddy could see what he's paying for, he'd have me covering HEW for the rest of my life."

It was just after nine o'clock when we saw Morgan, who was careful to pause and turn on a brighter light in the sitting room, and one in the library, behind us, before he came onto the verandah. We were prepared by the increase of illumination for the sound of the screen sliding open, and turned where we sat.

With the light behind him, it was difficult at first to distinguish his features. But he was a small man, compactly built, probably slight in his youth and now in his years reaping the benefit of that, looking more powerful than stout with his additional poundage. He wore a white shirt and white trousers and sandals. "Gentlemen," he said, in a low but cordial voice.

"Mister Morgan," Andrew said, approaching him. They shook hands. "I'm Collier," he said. "This is Daniel Wills."

Close up, now, I could see that Henry Morgan had certainly once been handsome. His face was well formed and unmarked. He had a full head of white hair, and a closely trimmed white moustache, and a firm jawline. "Sir," I said, extending my hand.

He ignored it. He came right up to me and grasped me by the biceps. He was shorter than I, by a good four inches, so that he had to look up at me, and his eyes, full of black light, scanned my features intently while he smiled. "Compton," he said. "I can't tell you, after all these years, what a pleasure this is. Your father was very dear to me, very dear."

He released me, then, and turned back to Andrew. "I knew your father only briefly," he said. "A tragedy. But your mother, of course, I knew quite well, and as we all did, I loved her."

He stood back from us then. "Well, well," he said, "an old man coming full circle, up from his nap in a dry season, tell me: what can the survivors of the last generation do to aid the captains of this?"

I was thoroughly charmed, until he said that. Then I realized that it was the setting which had until then tempered his flamboyance enough to make it tolerable. In Boston, I would have spotted him for the fraud that he was, at once. Just as Andrew had predicted, he was a wily and guileful old pirate, lurking away in his lavish hole in the wall, waiting to prey upon shipping that ventured too close to his lair. "This is certainly a beautiful spot, sir," I said. "How did you happen to hear of it?"

"Oh," he said, as the maid brought him a glass of white wine, and without being asked, removed our glasses and bought white wine to us, "— by the way, we'll be having dinner quite soon, and I thought you might wish to prepare your palates — for years I've made my home in the Caribbean. It seemed to reassure so many, who wished to think me a privateer, and found my audacity satisfying. For a long time I lived in the West Indies. I moved here when it became so easy for so many to visit the other islands, and in a way I am grateful for the signs of approaching release. There's a new hotel up at Biras Creek," he said, nodding his head to the east, "and the chartered boats grow more plentiful each year. I spend my working months in teeming cities, but the deserted ones, where I can rest, are becoming scarcer and scarcer. I know these islands quite well, actually, and I have always loved them."

His candor, as I came to think during the next forty-eight hours, was as deceitful as a clever falsehood, more so, in fact, because its practice enabled him to avoid so much as the effort to lie. Over a fine swordfish soup — the wine was Pouilly Fuissé, and it was abundant — cold lobster tails, a cold macaroni salad sprinkled with finely chopped pineapple, and cold green beans, vinaigrette, he established the pattern that he meant to follow during our discussions: he was so generous with the truth (or so it seemed), that one felt put in his debt, and thus disinclined to press him when he simply declined to provide information on what seemed to be an absurdly trivial point. As of course, they were trivial points, but he was preparing us to accept his silences on major questions, when they should occur. He broached no ground rules and requested no privileges of confidentiality. He simply trained us, or tried to, in the procedures that he wanted followed.

I did not, until we left that house around noon of our third day there, mention that view to Andrew. We had agreed, on the frightening airplane trip from San Juan, where we met at the airport, to exchange no confidences while we were at Morgan's house, on the suspicion (Andrew's) that it might very well be bugged. When I fairly exploded, as we started back up the mountain from the dock, again in the battered green van, Andrew shook his head slowly, negatively. Not until we were in the Dorado Wings aircraft, and warming up for takeoff back to San Juan, was he fully satisfied that no silent agents of Morgan's were around. "Keep in mind," he said, "that truck shows up when he wants it, and it's got a radio in it. Now look: he's been an international con man for upwards of fifty years. He didn't achieve that without learning a few tricks in how to limit what he tells people to what he wants them to know."

At table, on that first evening, Morgan suggested that we ought to begin by getting acquainted. He thought most of the burden was upon him, since he knew a good deal of our history from his friendship with our parents. "And, too, of course," he said, "I am not writing a story. So I will fill in the tedious details of my past."

He had been born, he said, in Brussels, in 1890, the third son of an export-import banking specialist employed as an independent contractor for Hagedorn Frères, a Netherlands banking house with offices in Paris, London, New York and the Dutch West Indies. Primarily of French descent — he had Anglicized his name from Henri — he attributed his surname to an Irish grandfather who had fought with Napoleon as a fugitive from his homeland. By the time he was ready to be sent down to school, his father had been placed in charge of Hagedorn's London office, and the boy was enrolled at Magdalene College, Cambridge.

"By then," he said, "with the Great War approaching, my father had prudently seen to the creation of a new Hagedorn firm in Zurich, had prevailed in his advice to consolidate all operations in Switzerland, and had with the same prescience exchanged our Belgian citizenship, as you would call it, for Swiss. What he labored to accomplish in nineteen-and-six paid large dividends for us when war broke out. No Hagedorn funds were impounded or confiscated, a circumstance for which the owners were appropriately grateful, and no Morgans, being citizens of a neutral country, were conscripted."

When he came down from Cambridge, in 1910, Morgan was sent to Zurich, and there, "in the gardens of the Alps, with the lakes shining and amidst the flowers," he spent the First World War. Learning the export-import banking business, inside and out.

"I was proficient at it," Morgan said, "but I did not enjoy it. It seemed that my tasks had principally to do with the manipulation of events and documents in order to achieve success for others.

"Now that will come as a surprise to you, I suppose," he said, "because, of course, I am aware that I am known primarily as a manipulator. But one cannot do much about his reputation. I am an entrepreneur, and by nineteen nineteen, I knew it. I was also restless, weary of the pastoral calm of Switzerland, beautiful though it is, and hungry, at twenty-six years, for a taste of life.

"My father objected strongly to my decision. But he acceded to my arguments of discontent, and to the inescapable logic of my argument that my younger brother, Frederick, something of a dullard, could handle the same job as well, in contentment, and needed it more. At last I was given his blessing.

"Among the Hagedorn clients," Morgan said, "was Vulcan Forge, Limited, a manufactury which made its products in Manchester, England, and did its business in London. Before the war, Vulcan had produced looms, presses, boilers, that sort of thing. During the war it had shifted production to components for war machines — the first primitive tanks, transport lorries, artillery caissons. Not a great market for that, once hostilities were ended, and Vulcan'd been a bit slow in retooling to resume production for its prewar markets.

"There was a penalty for that," Morgan said. "The firms that were prompt had captured the old Vulcan trade, and with superior machinery too, I might add. Vulcan awoke from its slumber to find itself outmatched in the markets, outmatched in design, and very much at a consequent disadvantage in financial circles, where it would be necessary to find the monies for modernization. They were very greatly alarmed, and so they should have been.

"I went to my father," Morgan said, "and I told him that this was clearly my opportunity. I asked him to request the directors at Hagedorn for permission to me to sever my ties with the firm, in order to undertake business for Vulcan, which would, of course, remain with Hagedorn after I left. With great reluctance, and considerable misgivings, my father agreed, and the deed was done.

"This was early in January of nineteen nineteen," Morgan said. "I had not married, and I had made a good living, and I had emulated the behavior of the people of my adopted country. So while I appeared to be taking a great gamble, and indeed, I was, I was in a much more secure position than I seemed to be, for I had savings, and could afford to gamble a little in order to win a lot.

"I returned to the people at Vulcan, and made them a proposition: working without salary or expenses, I would act as their sole representative, worldwide, to obtain new contracts for the company. They would pay me one-half of the net profits — it was a well-managed company, on the operational level, and net profits were substantial, when there were any profits at all — on all contracts which I negotiated during the first year; forty percent of net profits on contracts which I negotiated during the second year; and so on, declining to ten percent for the final year of a five-year contract.

"They were both pleased and taken aback," Morgan said.

"On the one hand, they had feared that I would seek an exorbitant salary and commissions. On the other, that I would demand an ownership interest. That I did neither, pleased them. Of course I would scarcely have sought an ownership share in a company in danger of going under, but they steadfastly denied to one another that it was in terrible trouble, and so overlooked that point.

"Still, when they thought about it, they were momentarily unwilling to afford me what I asked. For while they could reasonably expect no profits from my first year of operation as their agent, the heavy machinery business being a time-consuming thing to turn around, it was not lost upon them that whenever my agreements might be performed, they would owe me half of what they made on every one I developed in the first year. Forty percent the second, and so on.

"They protested. I reminded them that they lacked the funds to hire me at salary anyway, and that by my offer, I was shouldering some of their risk. At last we compromised: we entered into a four-year agreement, starting at forty percent, and working down from there."

Expansive in the candlelight, Morgan moved his chair back slightly as the maids cleared away the salad plates. A compote of fruit and kirsch was brought, and ponies of a clear raspberry brandy.

"I lost track of my own travels during nineteen nineteen," Morgan said. "Most of the countries which I visited, I visited twice, or more. And this was long before air travel, gentlemen. I was in France numerous times. Germany. Belgium, the Netherlands, Italy. Austria. Spain. To complete one venture, I visited Cairo three times. I was briefly in India, then Ceylon. I came at last to the United States, at the port of New Orleans, remained almost three months in your country, and at Christmas went to Havana, all but exhausted. There, in a club one evening, I met a man in a white suit, the friend of a friend of mine. We had one drink, and exchanged good wishes. Nothing more. A photograph was made. And it has haunted me ever since. That man was known as *Lupo*.

"During that entire year," Morgan said, "no more than fifteen or twenty percent of the agreements which I made for Vulcan were the sort of agreements which they had anticipated. They had expected me to sell their products, peddling obsolete heavy machinery in backward countries, to get their plants working again. But I sold first their processes, as obsolete as they were in England but not in Ceylon, and then the very tooling that the English technology had made obsolete, to the Ceylonese, in return for perpetual licensing fees. I sold their out-of-date practices and out-of-date equipment right out from under them, and when they protested, I asked them what they had been earning from idle tooling, and idle men.

"Then," Morgan said, "having cleaned out Vulcan's shops, and assured them of substantial profits from tooling and process sales, without any overhead for labor or materials, I surveyed the United States. Your technology was on a par with Britain's at least. There was no likelihood of palming off old hats to you; in most instances, your hats were better than ours.

"But," Morgan said, "if you do not find in an economy the opening to sell something that you do not want anymore, then it is time to look around to see if perhaps there is an opportunity to sell something that you haven't made before. It was that opportunity which I sought.

"I found it," he said, with considerable satisfaction. "Your technology was expanding so rapidly that your manufactury was having trouble keeping up with it. Additionally, it was spawning — and I have particular reference to the automobile — a huge and imperfectly grasped secondary and tertiary market, for materials such as asphalt, gasoline and rubber. So, in the last quarter of nineteen nineteen, I inquired of several manufacturers about whether storage tanks with seamless welds — which I knew Vulcan able to make, with minimal tooling, and at labor costs in Britain sufficiently lower than those in the States to offset shipping charges — might not last longer, and thus be cheaper, than the conventional sort. Before the year was out, I had obtained contracts for such tanks in a very tidy amount."

"How much?" Andrew said.

"A very tidy amount," Morgan said. "I had Vulcan retooling at favorable financing, to do very profitable work, and I had earned commissions in hand, from clearing out Vulcan's obsolete tooling, to enable me to spend my time in Havana reflecting on possible investments of my own. I would never, at least not for a very long time, abandon entirely my efforts to expedite the performance of Vulcan agreements made in nineteen nineteen, because even those not completed until the middle thirties continued to bring me forty percent of Vulcan's profits. I was constrained, to my deep sorrow, to cause an audit of Vulcan books a couple times just before World War Two, because I suspected that they had been holding out on my nineteen twenty, twenty-one and twenty-two commissions — and they had been — but it was still an appropriate time to turn my attention at least partially to longer-term personal investments.

"From that reflection," Morgan said, "and from ostensibly idle conversations which I had with fellow vacationers that holiday, I determined to consider a number of possible enterprises. One, at the time, seemed minor, both in terms of duration and annual profit, but worth pursuing nonetheless; after discussions with a number of gentlemen who were purchasing as many speedboats as they could find, I had determined to inquire into the availability of outmoded but seaworthy small freighters. Plying back and forth between Scotland and the three-mile limits, until Repeal, they easily returned their cost of purchase and operation, a very decent profit, and nearly all of their original value, to me, in scrap."

"I would imagine, sir," Andrew said, as the maids brought coffee and Havana cigars, "that you made a number of useful friends in that business, also."

"Indeed, sir," Morgan said, smiling again. "But whatever the business, that has always been the case. There is no such thing as a useless friend, or a harmless enemy. Or, if there is, it is safer to act as though there were not.

"But it was very difficult," Morgan said, "for the people at Vulcan, wretched ingrates that they were, to accommodate themselves to that or any other sensible understanding of commerce. Once they were on their feet, and doing well as a result of my efforts, they commenced to take umbrage at that, and certain other enterprises that I had undertaken."

"What other ones?" I said.

"Well," he said, "we will doubtless come to some of them."

"Involving my father?" I said.

"Compton," he said, most agreeably, "my only occasion to encounter your father, when I desired him to do something for me, was in the early nineteen twenties — and I honestly forget the date — when I wished to expedite the performance of certain contracts for Vulcan seamless tanks, with Standard Oil. I had heard reports that your father had an interest in expedition of such projects also. I went to see him, and conveyed to him certain information to which he was not privy. I do not know if he acted upon it, or if someone else acted upon it, thereafter. I lacked authority to do so, myself. All I know is that the bottleneck was removed, and the matter was resolved. Thereafter we saw each other from time to time, chiefly in

New York and Washington, always by the chance of having business with Standard, renewed old acquaintances, and went our separate ways. It was not until a few years before the Second World War that I had anything further, of, let us say, a business nature, to do with Cable. I would have preferred it to have been otherwise, but it was not. I simply had no legal work for him to do."

"When you resumed business contacts," Andrew said, "who initiated them? Was it you or was it Cable?"

"It was Cable," Morgan said. "It was in nineteen thirty-eight. We had met, by chance, in London and elsewhere, many times during the eighteen years or so that had elapsed since I had been in touch with him, but this was the first occasion since then that anyone wished anything to be done. I was in Singapore, and received a cable from my home office in Nassau, asking me to contact him, at Claridge's. I did so, and we agreed to meet there in a month."

It was late, then, and he was shrewd enough to know that he was growing old. He stood up, suddenly, and the large black woman appeared as though by standing he had summoned her up in a vision.

"Zeena," he said, "it's bedtime for old men. Please serve my guests on the verandah."

We had one drink of brandy and soda, and went to bed.

WE WERE UP at six-fifteen. There was old age compensation, it appeared, for naps in the afternoon and bedtime in the shank of the evening: together with the small brown lizards, striped white down the center of their backs, that watched me shower, attentively, from the sloping boards of the jalousies in the bathroom windows, Henry Morgan got up, and attended to a good deal of the day's business before the sun was high. From the library downstairs, not importunately, but insistently nonetheless, came "Stompin' at the Savoy," and "Bugle Call Rag," which brought me, at least, to the point of attentiveness required for full wakefulness when "Sing, Sing, Sing" came on.

We stumbled down the stairs, showered, shaved and fully dressed, but very far from completely alert. Exactly, of course, as he had desired it. We sat down greedily to orange juice, at six forty-five A.M. He was jovial, but I don't remember what he was being jovial about.

Promptly at seven, the woman appeared in a white caftan, with red, coarse stitching. She had reddish-blonde hair, long enough so that it fell to God knows where under the collar of her caftan, and a full body. She was a tall woman, not overweight at all. She had grayish-green eyes that glittered, high cheekbones, and a straight set to her lips. She addressed him in a language that I could not understand.

"This is Margarethe," he explained to us. "She is Norwegian," which perhaps she may have been, for all I know — she looked to be about forty, forty-five, in excellent trim — "and does not have any of our common language." That, of course, was a lie; we heard her addressing the cook in English in the kitchen, before we left. "She is my assistant now, since I have become too feeble for the continuous travel that my enterprises require. She says that I have been extremely rude to you, 'awakening your guests at your insane hours.' She arrived very late last night, from Saint Thomas.

"Forgive me," he said to us. Then he said something to her, in that other tongue, which I can only assume to have been the same thing. It did not soothe her, though. She clapped her hands, furiously, twice, and the large black woman appeared, on the double, bearing half a grapefruit. Margarethe went after it as though she had planned to kill it, in lieu of something else.

Morgan was completely undismayed. "You see," he said, "I am an eclectic soul. In my travels, so many times around this poor world, I have acquired tastes of extreme diversity. In food, in drink, in sport — I never missed a cockfight, willingly, when I chanced to be in Bangkok — and," he cast a glance sidelong at Margarethe "in women."

"You were never married, sir?" Andrew said.

"For several years, yes," Morgan said. "And but for my repeated and prolonged absences, they were happy years. She is dead now, for a long time. I do not care to talk about it further.

"From the United States," he said, "I took away, without paying any export duty, too, I might add, a taste for your music. The Dorsey brothers. Benny Goodman. I attended that concert, in nineteen thirty-eight, at Carnegie Hall, which Margarethe is so incensed at me for playing this morning. Glenn Miller. Paul Whiteman. Tony Paster. I had some small part to do with the arrangements to bring the King of Swing, as he was known then, to the Palladium. I made some money from it, and it was a bonus, because I would have done it for the music. One night, when I was in New York before the war, I held a gathering at a flat which I then leased, and obtained Lionel Hampton and his trio for the late evening entertainment.

"So you see," he said. "I play the music in the morning, because that is when I must do my business in Europe and the Orient, and the music helps me think. I am terribly sorry if I disturbed you, and I ask your indulgence."

Then he said something to Margarethe, which we were supposed to believe to be a recitation of the apology and justification we had just been treated to, in English. She snapped something back at him.

"She desires to know," he said, turning to us, "if my boorishness has been forgiven, on the condition that I not repeat it."

Andrew assured him that it was not boorishness, and that we had come neither to disrupt his household nor to interfere with his business. There was just enough edge in Andrew's voice to alert me to his anger at this charade. I have known Andrew a lot longer than Morgan had, but Morgan had been around a lot longer than I had, and I could not decide whether he perceived it. He addressed some remarks to her, which made her look up sharply from time to time, but did not cause her to answer. Then she returned her attention to the grapefruit, finished it, arose before any of us could have prepared for it, bowed, stiffly, and stalked off, still formally unintroduced. We did not see her again.

Apologetically, as though trying to ease the strain, as the eggs were served, Morgan said: "She is very tired. While I pay her well, and trust her implicitly, she is weary from traveling around the world at my behest. She has her own quarters, her own office, her own secretary, everything. She may, perhaps, be at that time of the month, eh?"

He seemed delighted with that possibility, and smiled companionably at us. "It was years ago, years ago indeed, gentlemen, when I first perceived the significant strategic advantages to be gained from the employment of women as assistants. The competitor always assumed that the employment was a masquerade for a sexual arrangement, or, in the alternative, took the employment relationship, to me, at face value, but dissipated some of his attention from business to an attempt to instigate a sexual liaison of his own. In either event, my bargaining position was improved, enough so that I was willing to make allowances for the periodic uselessness of such employees."

Nodding with satisfaction, he poured tea, and with both hands raised the cup to his lips. "I have always taken every available advantage," he said. "There were many who assumed that I was related to, and representing, the Morgans of New York. I never took the trouble to dissuade them. And, when asked directly, I made my truthful denials as unconvincing as possible."

"And what, exactly," Andrew said, "did all that get you, that you wouldn't've gotten anyway?"

"It's difficult to be sure," Morgan said. "One is never able to specify exactly what action of his was solely responsible for some happy development, because, in every instance that I have known, it was entirely plain that an accumulation of factors was responsible. Because I had an interest in Vulcan's international contracts, I acquired information about certain problems of Standard's, which was of interest to a perfect stranger, Cable Wills. I provided it to him, for reasons of anticipated mutual benefit which turned out to be justified. From that experience, Cable developed the opinion that I had access to sources and information which he lacked, that I was trustworthy and discreet, and that in times of exigency, might possibly be of service. I like to think I never disappointed him, or any other man who trusted me."

"How is it," I said, emboldened by an increasing dislike for this satisfied man, "that you contrived to remain at large so many years?"

"You mean," he said, smiling: "how did I stay out of prison?"

"More or less," I said, "if you want to put it that way."

Andrew started to say something, which Morgan chose to anticipate as an apology, and to wave aside. "No, no," he said, "it's a fair question. A hard question, because of its implications, but a fair one, and I will answer it.

"First," Morgan said, "I never intentionally did anything that was illegal, under the laws of any country in which I had business interests. As Compton here must grant me, I was careful always to obtain local counsel of the greatest acumen, and to follow to the letter the advice which I received. So, while envy and jealousy, arising in the hearts of opponents whom I bested, might very well have brought in their turn one investigation after another, it was evidently very difficult for even the most vengeful of prosecutors to establish a case against me. I was, in short, extremely careful, because while business can be conducted from the penitentiary, it can never be conducted well. My affairs have always required my full attention, and personal supervision. It was in my interest to avoid suspicion."

"But you didn't," Andrew said. "The Teapot Dome . . ."

"Ah, yes," Morgan said, "poor Mister Fall. But there, you see, is a perfect exemplar for my thesis: had I been culpable there, of any offense, surely I would have been hunted down for it. But the most that was ever proved of me — and it was proven only because I immediately came forward and quite cheerfully admitted it — was that I had favored the release of the Wyoming resources, in general, in order to obtain a favorable reaction in the costs of fuel for commercial shipping. I had so stated in a letter which I sent to Secretary Fall in response to a published report that he was contemplating such release. In that letter, I started my personal interest, but remarked also, again truthfully, that I believed the general economic effects would be advantageous to all.

"At his invitation," Morgan said, "I conferred with the Secretary in Washington, on my next visit. While it was a private visit, I can assure you that I did nothing more than reiterate my written views, and perhaps expand upon them. But I advocated no solicitation nor acceptance of bribes or any other consideration. Only because I was candid also, about that conference, when few others were willing to take the chance of divulging all that they had done, was I suspected of impropriety."

"Then that was rather reckless of you," I said. "Uncharacteristic poor judgment, wouldn't you say?"

"Hardly," Morgan said. "You must remember that this was early in my career. While it had begun auspiciously, very auspiciously, it required constant and careful attention. My Vulcan agreement was running out, and while my personal enterprises were prospering, they did not satisfy me. Those enterprises, by the way, were speciously cited by the Vulcan principals in a mean-spirited effort to repudiate my contract. It was short work, of course, to demonstrate to the court that while I had agreed to be their sole agent, I had not agreed to act solely as their agent, and they were assessed punitive costs for their rashness. But that enforced upon me the recognition which I had earlier possessed: that my future must, to be satisfactory to me, be grounded in an established reputation of my own, and not some precarious agreement with a small group of greedy men.

"In those circumstances," Morgan said, "with Britain and France staggered by their losses in the First World War, Germany in very questionable condition, and Russia still in the paroxysms of her recent revolution, the United States was clearly the market of opportunity for ambitious manufacturers and investors on the Continent. Since I had nothing to lose by the eventual disclosure of my communications with the Secretary, I had much to gain from assuring that those communications were reported."

"The reports made you look somewhat shady," I said.

"What you Americans call *shady*," Morgan said, smiling, "my principals term *influential*. It did not distress them, I assure you, gentlemen, that I had seen fit to express my views to a member of the Harding Cabinet. Still less were they put off by the hospitality with which my views were received."

"We use the root of that word, perhaps somewhat more pejoratively," Andrew said. "We call it: *influence peddling*."

Morgan leaned back in his chair now, grinning broadly.

"Ah," he said, "you Americans. I had some hopes for you during the Second War. I had some faint hope that perhaps you had at last closed your catechisms and determined to behave in the world of reality as the world of reality expects men to behave.

"Cable," he said to me, "by his actions gave me some encouragement in that belief. It was he, after all, who exerted himself to get in touch with me.

"And," Morgan said to Andrew, "I must confess that in consideration of your history, I am startled to hear such pieties from you."

Andrew's anger came up the back of his neck like a flag.

Morgan held up his left hand. "Pause yet awhile," he said. "You were not the scion of favored circumstances. Your father died honorably, but he had not lived, well, successfully, by the ordinary measure of worldly standards. I had great admiration for Sandy Collier's singular abilities, not to mention his extraordinary courage. He had his deficiencies, but he was a tenacious man, who could be trusted implicitly to carry out any assignment that fell to him. That was why I recommended him, when Cable asked for my advice.

"Still, in all," Morgan said, "his valor did not leave you favorably situated, as you must surely recognize. Yet today, at early middle age, you are able to look back upon a career that a man of much greater years would be hard put not to envy. Do you imagine that you accomplished this entirely upon merit?"

"I do my job very well," Andrew said, very hotly.

"Of course you do," Morgan said. "But, if you are honest with yourself, you must concede there are at least a hundred others, given your start, who would have done it at least passably well, but never got the chance because you had it."

"Sure," Andrew said, uneasily.

"Well," Morgan said, "your initial position with the Associated Press was the consequence of relationships developed by Cable Wills and Byron Price, who was General Manager of the Associated Press until nineteen forty-one, when President Roosevelt put him in charge of the Office of Censorship. Cable met Price through Elmer Davis at the Office of War Information, and he knew whom to call when you graduated from college and started looking for work. Is that *influence-peddling*, Mister Collier? And, if you say that it is not, please tell me how it differs from the real goods."

There was some silence. "That," Morgan said, his good humor ostentatious, "is the sort of enthymeme which for wearisome decades we in the international markets have been proposing to Americans. And it is the necessity for continuation of the practice which I hoped to have seen for the last time during World War Two.

"I did not see Cable on matters of mutual interest more than two or three times until after Repeal," Morgan said. "Those were points of great similarity to our initial meeting: separately, and for reasons and principals whom we did not identify to each other, we would find ourselves engaged in negotiations which disclosed information, and it would occur to us that perhaps there might be some advantage to be gained from sharing what we had learned.

"It was not difficult to arrange such conversations," he said. "Cable was in London frequently, representing, I gather, ALCOA and Westinghouse, working out reciprocal agreements with manufacturers and importers from the Continent. I offered to propose him for membership of the Garrick Club, of which I am a member, but he never saw fit to accept my offer. Still, we met socially from time to time, and in the late thirties, with Landings Jessup and Aubrey Gammage."

Morgan arose from the table now, and walked into the sitting room. "Perhaps we might have our coffee on the verandah," he said, "before I retire, again in obedience to my damnable physician."

He turned to face us. "Gentlemen," he said, "never get old. It is extremely inconvenient. The very qualities which you have depended upon, to make your life full, are inventoried by physicians, and then parceled out to you in small doses, on the express statement that you haven't much of them left, and must ration them. For years I was fully rested on three or four hours of sleep a night. Circadian rhythms meant nothing to me; I was as much at home in one hemisphere as the other, as comfortable with Indonesian food in my belly as I was with ortolans. Now everything must be considered before it is done, and reconsidered afterwards, and all agreements must be scrutinized for their operability in the event that my hearing, while striking the bargain, may not have been acute enough to apprise me that Time's wingèd chariot was closer than I thought. A ripe old age, indeed: when the fruit is ripe, it is ready to drop from the tree, and be *eaten*." Then he walked out of the room.

The coffee was waiting for us on a tray on the verandah. And it was dreadful, dark and with a bitter taste. He noticed my expression as I tasted it. "And there, at least," he said, "is one area in which I will grudgingly accord Americans superiority: no matter where you are in the United States, it is nearly always possible to obtain an agreeable cup of coffee. I have tried all possible measures. I have had American brands shipped in, and I have brought Jamaican and Colombian blends with me when I have returned. Yet somehow, no matter what I do, the beverage that is served is this, full of chicory, always scalded, and ordinarily the best advertisement for tea that one could possibly imagine." He set the cup down and sighed. "The trouble is that I have been, to that degree at least,

Americanized, myself. I no longer desire tea in the morning, and so I suffer this.

"As Hitler's intentions grew plainer and plainer," Morgan said, "if more plainness had been necessary, as it certainly was not, our social gatherings at the Garrick and at White's became more and more ponderous. Cable and Aubrey, having had no direct experience of the frustrations of military preparedness, began by chafing at the bit, Aubrey of course greatly restricted by his official position, Cable limited by the fact, as he saw it, that he had no official position. Landings viewed all matters quite morosely; as the son of a First Sea Lord, with some considerable firsthand recollection of what England had suffered before she armed, he was fatalistic about Chamberlain's positions. He did not approve of them, naturally, but neither did he truly consider that one sailor, two Americans and a merchant would reverse them over cards and port, before a fire. Landings quite endorsed your father's views," Morgan said to me, "and he certainly shared Aubrey's frustrations, but he was very saturnine when they began in optimism, and not of much use in cheering them up when they were reduced to pessimism.

"Now as I recall it," Morgan said, "the question of rubber did not really register on anybody until late in nineteen thirty-seven or so. And if I am correct, I was the one who first raised it, after a trip which had taken me through the Far East.

"The Japanese version of *Lebensraum* then was no secret," Morgan said. "Their presence was in Manchuria, and they were rattling sabers throughout the Pacific. Conceding that the Emperor seldom confided in me, I ventured the question one evening about what would happen if Germany and Japan embraced each other, with the Empire descending upon Singapore and spreading out from there.

"On his next visit to London," Morgan said, "Cable reported

that his informants projected a virtual shutdown of the American rubber industry. His figures indicated that the United States, the arsenal of democracy, required some five hundred thousand tons of crude latex every year, and that all but about ten percent of it came from areas now known as Malaysia. He had also taken the trouble to confer with some experts employed by his client, Standard, and on the basis of those discussions had learned to his dismay that there was almost no contingency planning on that subject.

"Oh," Morgan said, "there was no shortage of recommendations. There never is. I knew of at least a dozen processes, myself, for synthesizing rubber, and Cable's inquiries had yielded most of those and perhaps a dozen more. But none of us was sophisticated enough in that field to know whether there was much among them to make one choose a given method over another, what raw materials they required, costs, sophistication of technology required, or anything else, really.

"Now you inquired, a little earlier," Morgan said, "how I have managed to remain at liberty, for all these years. And this may be a second reason: I have repeatedly made myself useful to others, who had nothing to pay me for my expertise. In this instance, as Aubrey and Cable agonized, and Landings sat by rather stupidly, shaking his head at the frenzies of those innocents who proposed to save the world from the Nazi holocaust by their own personal efforts, I was able to propose the name of a reliable scientist conversant with the field, with whom they might consult.

"That," Morgan said, "would have been Felix Bartle, a tutor in chemical engineering during my days at Cambridge. I never studied under him. We became acquainted at darts, in the evening."

"My grandfather," Andrew said.

"Your grandfather," Morgan said. "A retiring man, but a

brilliant one. Aubrey, given his position, could not approach him, of course, lest he seem to be in contravention of that quaint American notion which excludes the military from participation in those civilian matters of overriding significance to the military. But Cable, as it then seemed, was at perfect liberty to talk with anyone he wished, and so went up to Cambridge.

"He returned," Morgan said, "smiling that triumphant smile of the American who has overcome the first and smallest of a numerous and increasingly enormous series of obstacles. Oh, how I dread to see that smile. Such disappointment follows it, so crashingly. Now we had the problem well in hand. The best means to synthetic rubber was *Buna-S*. Cable represented the American licensee, and from Felix he'd obtained the name of still another company, small but possibly useful, which was also experienced with the substance, butadiene. In gratitude for my assistance, he advised me very strongly to look into the feasibility of purchase of the Rachel Fletcher Paint Company, in Wheeling, West Virginia.

"And, now," Morgan said, rising and glancing at his watch, "I will do, on orders, what I should have done then, in good judgment, and go to bed." He nodded at us. "I will see you gentlemen at luncheon."

XIV

WE SAT on the little beach, Andrew and I, in the morning sunlight, and watched three sailboats working their way west in the channel between the coral reefs. The wind was gentle, but steady, and their great wings billowed full on the bright blue water. For a long time we sat without talking, occupied separately with sorting out what Morgan said, and was. Then, still both perplexed, we began, rustily, to work together on the thing, to talk, without the undercurrent of Andrew's animosity that had plagued our meetings for years.

"The first time I got involved in dealing with one of those old grizzled warriors," Andrew said, "I got a stiff lecture on my inexperience, and their complexity. Because I hadn't been around, thirty, forty years ago, I would never be able to understand what had happened to the people who were, or what their motives were, or how things that seemed clear-cut, black and white, now, were pretty confused, then.

"I didn't take it very well," Andrew said. "For one thing, I was not sitting there talking to him because I expected him to interpret the Scriptures for me. What I wanted was some straight answers to some straight questions. So I said that. 'Look,' I said, 'if I wanna go down to the red light district, and watch Enticing Lulu, I'll do it. If I want a whole hod of theology, I'll go see Reinhold Niebuhr.'

"Well," Andrew said, "I got about what you would've expected from that. From a grouchy old bastard, I made a perfectly furious old bastard, and the hell of it is, of course, now, I see that he was right.

"I go around," he said, "asking people questions, and I don't do it off the crack of the bat, either. I go in prepared, and I don't pull the pin unless I'm pretty sure that the thing's gonna go off when I throw it. But I still really don't know what went on, and I never really find out, either. What I get is what the guy I'm talking to, remembers, sometimes right and sometimes wrong, about what he was thinking when the other people that I'll never talk to were thinking other things.

"Now this guy," Andrew said, meaning Morgan, "is as wily as a leopard, and at least three times as fast, over short courses. And in places, he is trying to mislead me. In others, he's trying to confuse me, and in some, he's just plain flat out not talking. That stuff about my father?"

"He seemed sincere enough, then," I said.

"That's only because," Andrew said, "after all this time, he probably believes it. Maybe he's always believed it. I believed it for a long time myself. Then I saw something that made me wonder if maybe something'd been worked on me, and I started thinking about it, and now I don't believe it anymore."

I didn't understand, and I said so.

"There's a technique," Andrew said, "that only the real professionals use, because it takes careful planning and good co-ordination. The Nixon people used it, but they didn't do it very well. Not nearly as well as some others you could think of, and I could name.

"My kind of work," Andrew said, "can only be done by a hard-ass, a real ball-breaker, and all of us real ball-breakers know it. Oh, we got the eyes narrowed to slits and the thin compressed lips, and when you tell us something, by Jesus, the fact you're telling us doesn't make it so, and we're gonna look into it.

"Now that gives you a funny kind of perspective on things," he said. "It reverses things. If somebody comes right out and says it, that's the same thing as a press release, and the odds are that the guy's lying to you. Which, in most instances, he is. The minute he closes his mouth, you start checking around, see if you can catch him out, and most times, you can and you do and you let him have it, right in the brisket.

"The ones that're really clever," Andrew said, "know that. So they plan things out, and when they know you're gonna go looking for the truth, and they don't want you to know it, the first thing they do is salt the mine with the lie they want you to believe. They do that by telling the lie to some guy that they figure you're gonna talk to, who doesn't know it's a lie: he really believes it's the truth.

"Then," Andrew said, "they dream up another lie, not quite as good but okay if you happen to be really dumb, and go for it.

"These're not what you'd call barefaced lies," Andrew said. "Don't let *me* mislead you. The worst of them is always plausible, and contains some truth. Usually, quite a good deal. The corroborative stuff, for example: if they say there was a meeting, and the fellow was there, you can call up the Saint Regis Hotel and get their records, and by God there always was a meeting there that day, and your guy was a registered guest. They never put something in, when they set up the diversionary tactic; they save that for later. What they do is leave something out, such as that one of the other guys at that meeting was a notorious bagman, coordinating payoffs. If you don't know whom to look for, you'll never find him.

"All right," Andrew said, "let's assume you get some reason to think there's something very funny going on. They throw you the first one, and you spit it out. Now, if they set it up right, you're gonna work like a bastard, until you finally come to the guy they've got primed to tell you the fallback lie, and after you worm it out of him, you'll think you've got the truth, and go with it. There's so many whores around, that'll believe anything anybody tells them, that the rest of us don't believe anything, and so we're even bigger suckers for a planted story, because if we really had to scout around for it, and work for it, when we get it, we believe it.

"That," Andrew said, "and I'm convinced of this, that is what my mother did to me."

"Good God, Andrew," I said.

He shook his head. "God's honest truth," he said. "I'm pretty sure I know why she did it, and at least at first, I could understand it. And I don't condemn her for doing it. She thought she had good reasons, and she accepted the reasons that the other people gave her. Her motives were all right. But she was still doing it, and doing it to me, her own son.

"There *was* a man named Sandy Collier," Andrew said. "I looked into that a long time ago. He grew up in the Five Points, in the twenties, and hung around with the wrong kind

of guys, and then he was in Chicago when Capone was fighting Dion O'Banion. He was on the wrong side, of course. Then
he went back to New York and got himself tied up with some
guy that had a connection with Johnny Torrio in Chicago, and
that's where he stayed until he went to Sing Sing in nineteen
thirty-five, a year before Dewey put Salvatore Lucaina in for
running hookers, for doing a guy in or something. Lucaina was
Lucky Luciano. Charlie Lucky was that fellow that teamed
up with Meyer Lansky, to pull the murders that got called the
Nights of the Sicilian Vespers. Which was when Lupo the
Wolf packed it in, and the Mob was up for grabs. Wanna
guess who the Lupo was, that Morgan met? There is no question that there was a man named Sandy Collier, or that he was
a very bad actor.

"Collier," Andrew said, "got out of Sing Sing in nineteen
thirty-seven, and nobody seems to know what brought that on,
either. His file is missing. He apparently left the country, and
by nineteen forty-three, he was dead.

"He did not die at El Alamein," Andrew said. "He wasn't
within a thousand miles of Rommel's Afrika Korps at any time
in his whole life."

"Well," I said.

"Well," Andrew said, "if he wasn't fighting with Mont-
gomery when he bought the ranch, my mother must've known
it."

"Right," I said.

"So," Andrew said, "why did my mother, and your father,
tell me that he was?"

"I don't know," I said.

"Well," Andrew said, "I think I do. Or at least, I thought I
did, and I'm still not sure I don't."

"Andrew," I said, "she was married to the man."

"So far as we know," he said. "Those records were destroyed,
too, in the bombing."

"But why would she lie about that, assuming that she lied about anything?" I said.

"Because her father was alive then, too," Andrew said.

"Tell him," I said, "that she'd married a killer?"

"She didn't have to tell him that," Andrew said. "All she had to tell him was that she was married to somebody, and produce a warm body that was male and would agree with her. That would explain me."

XV

At LUNCHEON we enjoyed cold chicken and a Chablis on the verandah. Andrew was energetically self-contained, and Morgan was expansive.

"Cable," Morgan said, "was unusual for an American, in the economy of his motion. In many respects, he was the quintessential American, ebullient, filled with enthusiasm, but when he recommended a course of action, particularly in those days, on the ground that he had other things in mind which would materially enhance its likelihood of success, we soon learned to listen to him.

"I did as he recommended and requested," Morgan said.

"Through intermediaries, I negotiated the purchase of the Rachel Fletcher Paint Company."

"And made a lot of money off it," Andrew said.

"As a matter of fact," Morgan said, "I never realized so much as a reasonable return on the investment. While Cable was certainly correct in his view that the company had experience with butadiene, he was utterly mistaken about the response he predicted from his client, Standard, once the primary importance of the process was known. When the *Buna-S* process was broken loose, many companies gained access to it, and while Rachel Fletcher was one of them, it was of minimal significance. I sold the company, more than twenty years ago, to a subsidiary of Sofina, and that's the last I've heard of it."

Andrew was visibly disappointed. Morgan saw it. He leaned forward, over the wreckage of the chicken. "Operation Violet continued for the rest of the war," he said. "There were probes in Peenemunde, in the submarine pens in Norway, and some enterprises in the Baltic. I *understood*," he said, "that Cable, through *Predecessor,* arranged some coordination with the Generals seeking to kill Hitler. I understood that because I was the go-between for certain meetings outside Zurich. And I know," he said, "that your father, Andrew, was killed by the Abwehr after successfully completing a mission in Denmark, in nineteen forty-two."

"Do you know what it was?" Andrew said.

"It was a suicide mission," Morgan said. "He was recruited for missions of assassination, and he accepted one. The target was an obscure rocket scientist, whose specialty was deuterium. Heavy hydrogen. I knew neither the significance of his work, nor the circumstances of his death. I do know that he died, and that Sandy Collier killed him."

I do not mean now, or ever, to blink Andrew's very real acumen. He can be an unpleasant man, and certainly his suspiciousness verges on the pathological; at the same time, para-doxically, he can, almost by force of will, convince himself of some premise so farfetched, and so devoid of supporting evi-dence, as to strike the disinterested observer as utter fantasy. So, as I told Ellen, when Andrew declared, as we left the island, two days later, that the last piece of hard information, whether true or false he could not say, that Henry Morgan gave us, was that statement about Sandy Collier.

"The rest," Andrew said, "was smoke. Smoke and Saint Elmo's fire, iron pyrites and rhinestones. You go in expecting to see a reenactment of the crime, and all you get's a sudden, small movement behind the drapes, and there's the body on the floor in front of you. Well, maybe that's the way it did happen. Maybe there wasn't anything else to see, it was all done so quickly and so well. But maybe, too, it wasn't really done so well, when it was done the first time. Maybe the victim put up a hell of a tussle, and had to be hit with a hatchet, and when it was over there was blood all over the place: you'll never know, when they've had more'n thirty years to get the place cleaned up, and the story straight."

What plagued him, as I told Ellen, was the helplessness of a seer persuaded of the validity of an undemonstrable proposi-tion which, if it had been demonstrable, would solve every-thing. I have seen such frustration, many times, in younger associates encountering in my specialty the manifold, cumber-some and tedious complications which attend the registration of a public stock issue. While they have a grasp of the theory of Securities and Exchange regulations, and while there is no gainsaying their native intelligence, they are simply unpre-pared, and therefore appalled, by the sheer volume of tiresome work entailed by compliance with those regulations. Soon they commence to mourn for a simpler life, and then to yearn for a lodestone that will bring it to them, and that is when they bear watching, because they will seize upon any pretext to enable them to escape the tedium, most often by some brilliant stroke which will, in the end, get us all indicted.

"No," she said, levelly, "what bothers Andrew is a lot more personal than that."

I did not know what she meant. She was very reserved when I returned from the trip, standoffish and extremely controlled.

"Nothing," she said, "has ever turned out quite the way that Andrew expected it to. Danielle, for example."

"Danielle," I said, "evidently gave him some reason to suspect her. But that, in a way, is my point. As impulsive as he is, he acted upon his suspicions. That's what he's done with Dad, and that's what he's done with Morgan, and all the rest of it."

"Why does he suspect your father?" she said.

I had not meant to bring that up. "He's got this rather bizarre idea in his head," I said, "almost like a fairy tale. He rejects the facts of his lineage. He simply will not have it. He is doing now with his paternity what as a child he did with Christmas presents: comparing his to mine, preferring mine, and deciding to annex it for himself. Andrew believes that he is my half-brother. I'm sure of it, although he's never said it."

"He did have a rather unusual childhood," she said.

"Unusual," I said, "to the extent that Dad's simple kindness prompted him to provide employment and shelter to a woman and her son, because she had served him and the country well, at considerable danger to herself. Unusual, to the extent that Dad took responsibility out of generosity for a child who otherwise would not have had much to look forward to, and situated him to obtain substantial advantages.

"Look," I said, "Andrew is a resourceful man. Life is an extremely random business. He would have prospered, surely, without Dad's interventions. But not as soon, and certainly not as much.

"He is also a proud man," I said. "To avoid gratitude, he has resorted to a distortion of a charitable act, years of charitable acts, into years of expiation of a hidden sin, so that instead of facing me as the beneficiary of advantages that my father allocated to him, as generously, at least as generously, as he saw to my welfare, he confronts me as an injured party, still somehow responsible, now that Dad is dead, for perpetuation of a secret shame."

"Well," she said, "suppose it was true. Would your father have admitted it?"

"Ellen," I said, "you knew the man. He was totally upright. He scarcely ever drank. His work was his life. His reputation was impeccable. There never would have been such a thing to admit, because he never would have so transgressed. He was not a passionate man."

"He was a willful one," she said.

"Determined," I said, and I remembered the picture I had found in his safety deposit box. It was inscribed in black ink, protected by two pieces of corrugated cardboard, and the figure in it was in the fullness of his powers, the hat raked back, the spectacles lowered just a bit on the bridge of the nose, the confident smile and the cigarette, in his holder, at the jaunty angle; it must have been taken two or three years before it was inscribed: *For Cable Wills, with the lasting gratitude of his beloved country, FDR.* "A determined man and a resolute one," I said, "but not an intemperate one."

"He was a spy," she said.

"Oh, nonsense," I said. "He accepted certain missions for his country. He did what any other American would do. After the war, he continued informally to serve the government, when he was asked to do so, and when he could. And that was all."

"That's not what he told Andrew," she said.

"I don't know what he told Andrew," I said.

"Well," Ellen said, "neither do I, for sure. But I know what he told Danielle, your father told him. And he's told the same thing to Deirdre, for the same reason, I gather. He told them that your father, one night in Washington when they were having dinner, seemed on the brink of telling him something, then pulled back, and finally said: 'Andrew, I was puzzled for a long time by the way that other men behaved. My father, the people in the firm, the men who were my clients. Then, as I grew older, I began to understand that my actions were equally incomprehensible to them, and must be so, because often they were inexplicable by me, and then I was at peace, and some day, you will be also.' And that was all he would say."

"He took an interest in Andrew," I said.

"Compton," she said tiredly, "Compton, Danielle and I had our little talk, a long time ago. You screwed Danielle. I know it. And she conceded nothing, but then, she didn't need to. Ted Fullerton gave it away at least a dozen times, because he's fairly stupid, and it was the only explanation for everything, that made all the pieces fit together."

"Ellen," I said.

"No," she said, "it doesn't matter. It didn't matter when I learned of it, because it had stopped, and your Dad had done what he could do, to make things right, and I accepted those things, knowing why he did them, what he hoped to accomplish. What he wanted. So," she said, "I gave it to him. I know, Compton," she said, "I *know* what you did. I've known for a long time." Then she stared at me. "And your Dad knew, too.

"Now," she said, "you have to give him what he wanted, too, even though he's dead. It doesn't matter, Compton. It probably never mattered. If Andrew believes that, and I am sure he does, part of the reason he believes it is that your father, for good reasons of his own, decided to permit him to believe it, and did so, for you, because it meant that Andrew would do what your father, and I, desperately wanted."

"Ellen," I said, "Andrew, Andrew has a full head of hair. You've seen him. What he wants to believe is one thing. What is true is another."

"Compton," she said, "male pattern baldness has to be transmitted through the mother. Her genes can block the male genes that cause it."

$$\boxed{\text{XVI}}$$

My soliloquy, as Dad had written it, is still in his desk, which I moved out of Milton and kept for myself when we sold the house. By our family custom, it was read at his service without any elaboration except the extension of my thanks to those who attended.

In retrospect, he wrote, *it has all seemed very orderly, a progress through the years, carefully arranged, first bringing me here, where I was meant to be, and then in proper course, to other things. I have experienced the fidelity of friends, the love of family, the respect of colleagues and the fruition of my talents, all together with that best of human things, the agreeable belief that I was useful in my time.*

And yet, it was not orderly, except that so many labored so to make it. As I, in my turn, labored also, to bring to a chaotic world some minor betterment, to leave things improved over the condition in which I found them, to comfort the afflicted, succor the fallen, and assuage the grief of the bereaved. In that, I failed.

I do not grieve for that, though I regret it. It was all inevitable, once I began from where I did, saying not: The struggle naught availeth, I chose instead to begin in my youth with the admonition of the aged Ulysses to his crew, and demanded of my friends that they take oars, and smite the sounding furrows, for the foredoomed purpose that we sail beyond the baths of all the western stars, until we die.

I did enjoy your company, and the company of those now gone before me, whom I join.

Andrew, from Henry Morgan and the rest, obtained no publishable story, and went on to other things. When I had written this, I thought that I should show it to him, so I sent it to him with a note, that I had tried to tell the truth, and all of the story, and would appreciate his comments. I had titled it *Predecessor Violet*. This is what I received in return:

When Cable started representing Westinghouse, I guess it must have been, he wrote, *he evidently got a lot of equipment and stuff. At least it was there, when we were growing up, and I remember the phonograph playing, whenever he was home.*

There was one song that he particularly enjoyed. At least he played it all the time, scratchy and noisy as the old shellacs were.

Aubrey Gammage died a week ago. You may have seen the obits, and they were pretty long, too. The one in the Times *was what caught my eye. It said that he was active in the OSS, during World War II, and later in the CIA. It said, and this is* what made me remember: "Gammage was often described as the principal agent in a far-flung program of industrial sabotage and trade sanctions mounted against the Nazis in World War II. He invariably denied it, admitting only his involvement in a few small operations. 'The control,' he said, 'was Dreamland.'"

That was what did it, Andrew wrote. I could remember that record: "Meet me in Dreamland, sweet dreamy Dreamland. There let my dreams, come true." The Operation was one of many, in all likelihood. The operative who began things was Predecessor, because she came before, and that was my mother. The other code names were for convenience. As were many things.

I lack the diplomatic services of Daniel Cable Wills. I therefore will be blunt. Deirdre and I expect to be married, next month. We will live here. So far as I know, Creighton Labs does not have an office in the District. Ted Fullerton, for all I know, is dead. If he is not, nevertheless, do not invent a new one, or use the old one again. Because, as I lack Dad's diplomatic proficiency, so also am I excused, now that he is dead, from considering how what I'd liked to have done then, will affect him. If there is a next time, I will do it.

I think you did what you said you tried to do. I don't think you meant to, but you did.

Deirdre sends regards.

And that was when, at long last, I knew that Andrew was insane.